Holiday Sorrow

JANE BLYTHE

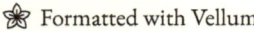 Formatted with Vellum

Acknowledgments

I'd like to thank everyone who played a part in bringing this story to life. Particularly my mom who is always there to share her thoughts and opinions with me. My wonderful cover designer Amy who did an amazing job with this stunning cover. My fabulous editor Lisa for all the hard work she puts into polishing my work. My awesome team, Sophie, Robyn, and Clayr, without your help I'd never be able to run my street team. And my fantastic street team members who help share my books with every share, comment, and like!

And of course a big thank you to all of you, my readers! Without you I wouldn't be living my dreams of sharing the stories in my head with the world!

CHAPTER

One

February 14th
10:57 P.M.

There were a million reasons why this was a bad idea.

Yet Ashlyn Davidson didn't tear her lips away from the man setting her body alight with a single kiss.

Maybe it was the fact that her brother was married now, while she didn't even have a man she could bring to the wedding as her plus one. Maybe it was because in less than a month she would be thirty and she hadn't achieved all the things she thought she would by the time she entered her fourth decade. Or maybe it was her new red hair color giving her extra confidence, but she was going to go for it.

Consequences be damned.

After all, what was the worst thing that could happen?

"You sure about this?" the man, with his hands firmly gripping her backside, asked as he pulled back enough to examine her expression.

Detective Grant Bull. Ashlyn wasn't so desperate that she'd have a one-night stand at her brother's wedding and not even know the guy's name. They'd been chatting all evening, she knew he was forty, a widower with two kids, and one of her new sister-in-law's colleagues. He had a great smile, kind eyes, just the right amount of scruffy beard to be wildly attractive, had been attentive and respectful, and he'd made her laugh, something she thought she couldn't do because she was so guilty about being jealous of her brother.

Donovan deserved all the good things in the world, and his new wife, Jessica, and stepson, Freddie, were just that. But she needed to do something wild and spontaneous, and a one-night stand with a sexy cop was just that.

"Never been more sure about anything in my life," Ashlyn assured Grant.

"Thank goodness, because I've been dying to taste you since I laid eyes on you."

With that, Grant spun her around, his knuckles trailing across her skin as he unzipped the back of her little black dress. Letting it pool at her feet, he helped her step out of the material, then spun her again so she was facing him. The arousal in his eyes was echoed by the tent in his pants, and her own arousal thrummed through her system.

Leaning in, his fingers skimmed her sides as he reached around her to unhook her bra. Ashlyn had always been a little embarrassed about her breasts because they were pretty small, but the way Grant's gaze seemed to darken quickly chased the feeling away.

"Perfect," he murmured as he grazed the calloused pad of a thumb over one of her nipples, making it harden.

"Can't help but notice things are a little unbalanced," she said, her gaze traveling his still suit-clad body.

"Hmm, they sure are," he said, amusement dancing in his eyes as he scooped her up and tossed her onto the bed.

Landing with a bounce and a giggle, Ashlyn had no time to think because Grant was right there, grabbing her panties and easing them down her legs. Her ridiculously high heels also came off, landing somewhere in the room, and she couldn't have cared less where.

"Good thing your brother and Jessica decided to get married at a hotel," Grant said as he nudged her legs apart and settled between them.

"Yeah, otherwise we would have had to get in a car and drive somewhere." That would have been more than enough time to have talked herself out of this.

With the first swipe of his tongue across her already wet center, Ashlyn knew she would have spent the rest of her life regretting missing out on this moment. Grant turned out to be some sort of tongue wizard. She'd never really been all that interested in having a man's mouth on her like that. It wasn't bad, but it had never been good.

Well, this went from good to amazing in about half a second flat.

Using nothing more than his tongue and his lips, he licked and nipped and suckled her toward a lightning bolt of pleasure. It zapped through her with strength she'd never felt before, and she hoped the room next door was empty because otherwise they would have for sure heard her screams of pleasure.

By the time she floated back down to earth, Grant had stripped out of his clothes and was rolling on a condom. There was something more than arousal in his eyes as he looked down at her, and she forced herself not to examine it too deeply.

One night.

That was all this was supposed to be.

All it could be, really.

"So beautiful," he told her as he leaned down to ravish her mouth with a fiery kiss, before he grabbed her hips and flipped her onto her stomach. Climbing onto the bed behind her, his hands closed around her hips once again, lifting them off the bed, and she felt him nudging her entrance.

As though he wanted to give her one last chance to back out, he didn't press inside her, and as desperate and needy as she was, that just wasn't good enough. Pushing back enough to take his tip, she moaned in delight at the stretch as his rather impressive length edged inside her.

"Okay, beautiful," Grant said with a chuckle, "I hear you loud and clear."

This wasn't a position Ashlyn had ever tried before, and she was unprepared for the delightful sensations as the tip of Grant's erection brushed across that magical spot inside her as he thrust into her.

His grip on her hips was almost bruising, not that she cared, and he set a relentless pace. One she was more than happy to meet, even if it did feel awkward at first, thrusting backward while on her hands and knees.

Their moans tangled together, heat flushed through her body, and when one of his hands left her hip to reach between her legs and press against her bud, she came with another scream that she was pretty sure had to have been heard by the whole floor.

Pleasure eventually faded, and her body, drowsy from two backto-back orgasms, sank down against the fluffy pillows. Grant moved with her, still buried inside her, and the weight of his body pressed lightly against hers, had her worrying she'd made a major miscalculation on her ability to be a one-night stand sort of girl.

CHAPTER
Two

March 23rd
  7:08 A.M.

They were going to be late.

He hated to be late.

Something Grant knew he should have gotten over by now, because ever since his fifteen-year-old daughter Lindsay hit the teenage years, they'd been late to school. Two years later, he thought she'd have mastered the art of applying her makeup and choosing her outfit for school, but unfortunately, that had never happened.

Still, he could live in hope. She'd be finishing her freshman year in just a couple of months, then there were only three more years to go until his baby would be graduating high school and moving on to her next big adventure.

Where did the time go?

Seemed like just yesterday he was watching his wife carry their newborn daughter into the nursery for the first time. Now Lindsay was fifteen, his son Kevin was twelve, and it had been nine years since his wife died in childbirth along with their second daughter, who he had wound up calling Lara, the same name as her mother.

Almost a decade of being a single parent had left him feeling like he'd missed out on a whole lot of living. Raising a three-year-old and six-year-old, grieving, trying to help his kids grieve, working, building a career, taking care of the kids and the house, and all the chores that needed to be done, didn't leave much time for anything else.

It didn't leave much time for any*one* else.

Like they did more and more these days, his thoughts drifted to the sexy redhead he'd met at a colleague's wedding over a month ago. Ashlyn Davidson was the first woman to catch his eye since he lost his wife. The first woman to make him feel like a man again, instead of just a dad and a cop.

Both of those roles he loved, there was nothing more rewarding than raising kids, and becoming a detective was everything he'd wanted since he was in middle school.

But he was more than a dad and a cop.

He was a man, and he was only mildly embarrassed to admit that the pair of panties Ashlyn had left behind that night were sitting upstairs, hidden in his sock drawer. Over the last five weeks, he'd gotten them out more than once and gotten himself off by wrapping them around his length and using his hand.

Before Ashlyn, there had been no getting himself off. Sex had been the furthest thing from his mind while he was just struggling to survive each day and the load of work that came with it.

Was he ready to move on?

The thought came out of nowhere and was followed by a rush of guilt as he glanced over at the large family portrait that hung above the fireplace. It was the last photo he had of his wife. In it, Lara was pregnant with baby Lara, the baby bump obvious as she'd been around seven months along. Lindsay's hair was perfectly braided, something he'd never quite learned to do, and Kevin was grinning at the mother he barely remembered like she was the center of his world.

Which was exactly what Lara had been.

The center of all their worlds.

But she was gone now, and despite the guilt, as he looked at her bright smile, he knew that she would have wanted him to find happiness again if he could. Grant wasn't saying that Ashlyn was the woman he would wind up being happy with, but he couldn't deny that time had dulled his loss enough that he was ready to look for love again.

A clatter on the stairs had him turning his head as his daughter finally made her way down them. Lindsay was the spitting image of her mother, and while looking at her had intensified the ache in his chest in those early days when his grief was still so raw, now he loved that his daughter was taking after her mother in every way.

"Glad you could finally grace us with your company," he drawled.

"Dad." She sighed in that way only a teenager could. "I'm like eight minutes late. Relax. It's not a big deal."

Being told to relax by one of his kids always made him smile, reminding him of all the times he'd tried to get them to relax when they were throwing tantrums and being typical rowdy kids. Despite the grief and all the work it had been wrangling two small children and balancing his career and the house, there had been a lot of good times. A lot he wished he had been able to share with Lara.

"Ready to go, Kev?" he called out to his son, who was playing some video game, cars darting around on a track on the television screen.

"One more minute," Kevin called back.

And this was exactly how eight minutes late turned into thirty in the blink of an eye.

Like clockwork, Lindsay glanced down at her outfit, a furrow forming between her brows. "If Kevin isn't ready yet, I might just run back upstairs and change my shoes."

"Lindsay," he groaned. Why did this happen every day? Getting his kids to coordinate their departure seemed as impossible as building a city on Mars. Lindsay took too long to get ready, so Kevin played video games, so Lindsay decided she had time to go and change something in her outfit, so Kevin started another race, and the cycle went on until he put his foot down and insisted he was leaving, and if they weren't ready they could walk to school.

"Relax, Dad. It won't take long," Lindsay told him as she hurried back upstairs.

"I'm ready," Kevin announced, looking over his shoulder. When he didn't see his sister, he turned his attention back to his game. "If Linds isn't ready yet, I have time for one more race."

Grant's groan turned into laughter. As much as his kids had the ability to drive him crazy, he wouldn't change a thing about their lives together.

Except maybe one day, adding a pretty redhead to their busy lives.

CHAPTER

Three

May 9th
    2:31 P.M.

Well, her thirtieth birthday had come and gone, and Ashlyn still hadn't been able to get a certain sexy cop out of her mind.

It had been almost three months since Donovan's wedding, and she'd thought that all thoughts of Grant Bull would have long since faded.

Yet they hadn't.

If anything, they seemed to grow more vivid the more she replayed their night together. Each brush of his fingertips against her skin seemed seared into her memory. How big he'd felt inside her, how perfect, it wasn't something she could get past. Every time she tried to get herself off with her fingers or a toy, she couldn't seem to manage it. She'd get so close, but she just couldn't fall over the ledge.

Seemed Grant had ruined her body for anyone—anything—that wasn't him.

Too bad nothing more could ever come of that one amazing night. If she'd thought there was a chance, she would have left him with her number when they finally finished up round six of sex in the shower and reluctantly pulled their clothes back on. Or she would have sucked it up, ignored the embarrassment, and asked Jessica for Grant's number.

But Grant was a widower who was still in love with his late wife. Plus, he had two kids who were the center of his world. He wasn't looking for a relationship, and since one-night stands aside, she was, they just weren't compatible.

With a sigh, she headed out of Eat Dessert First, the restaurant that her mom owned and ran. While she was the youngest of her mom's four kids and didn't really remember a lot from before her mom met and fell in love with a billionaire, she still knew they were extremely lucky. They had everything they could ever want or need, nothing was off the table. She'd been lucky enough to be able to pursue her dreams and build her own exclusive custom jewelry line, but the one thing she wanted more than anything else was something money could never buy.

Love.

A relationship like her mom and stepdad had. The real thing. True love. A happy ever after.

That's what she craved more than anything else.

Of course, there were plenty of guys who wanted to be with her because of her money, but she didn't want that. A loveless marriage would just wind up crushing her poor little romantic heart.

Glancing at the restaurant's back door, she tried to picture how it must have looked last Christmas when Jessica put Donovan in handcuffs. At the time, her now sister-in-law hadn't realized who Donovan was, and that he was trying to break in because mom had locked her keys inside, so she'd thought she was arresting a burglar.

Now the story was told with laughter, and honestly, Ashlyn just loved it. It was so romantic, and while things hadn't been smooth sailing for the couple, they were now happy and in love. She was pretty sure it wouldn't be all that long before Freddie became a big brother, and while she loved her brother very much, his new family, too, she was still struggling a little with the whole jealousy thing.

"Which is not nice," she reprimanded herself as she headed for her car.

It wasn't like she wanted to feel this way, because she absolutely did not. It made her feel like the worst sister in the world. She was genuinely happy for her big brother, she didn't want him not to have built the amazing life he had for himself. She just kept wondering when she was going to get that same chance at happiness.

Or if she ever was.

Lost in thought as she was, Ashlyn didn't realize anyone was behind her until she felt a body step up close.

Too close.

Quickly spinning around, she took a stumbling step backward when she saw a man standing there. He wore black jeans and a black hoodie with the hood pulled down low, covering most of his face. There were stains on his clothes, he smelled strongly of cigarette smoke, he had a scraggly beard, one of his shoes was missing, and she got a bad feeling.

"Oh, uh, did you need ... money?" she asked, her voice trembling a little. As well as running her own jewelry brand, she did a lot of work for charities, and she had no problem donating to homeless men and women, she did it often. But this man was giving off a vibe that she didn't like one little bit.

"Yeah, money," he snarled, lifting his head so she could catch a glimpse of more of his face. There was a coldness in his blue eyes that had her taking another stumbling step backward.

"I have money." Scrambling into her purse, she found the emergency money she always carried in case she came across someone in need. Handing over the crisp hundred-dollar bill, she took another step back. "If you need more help, please come to the shelter on Hemlock Street and tell them Ashlyn sent you."

As she tried to turn and hurry to her car, a hand darted out and grabbed hold of her elbow, yanking her backward and up against a hard chest. Her breathing accelerated, and everything she'd ever learned in self-defence classes flew from her mind, leaving her frozen in place.

"I think I have a better idea," the man growled, his breath hot against the back of her neck. "I think you're going to drive me to the bank, drain your account, and then give me all your jewelry. Might take your body, too." The hand not gripping her suddenly produced a knife, and he trailed the tip of it up one of her jean-clad thighs, then tried to nudge it between her legs, making her yelp in terror.

The man just laughed, then moved the knife so it was against her neck.

Never in her life had Ashlyn felt as absolutely vulnerable as she did in this moment.

"Let's go, princess, which one's your chariot?" the man demanded, and not knowing what else to do, she pointed to her Porsche and prayed for a miracle as he began to march her toward it.

CHAPTER
Four

May 9th
2:39 P.M.

Something was off.

Grant had stopped at the Eat Dessert First to grab something to bring home for the kids tonight. They'd both gotten great grades on their report cards, it was almost summer vacation time, and he wanted to do something to celebrate.

Then, as he'd been about to head inside, he'd noticed a woman in jeans and a bright pink sweater talking to a man in dark jeans and a black hoodie. Their interaction looked tense, and he wondered if it was some sort of drug deal. The guy could definitely be a dealer, and while the blonde looked too sweet and innocent to be caught buying drugs in a restaurant parking lot, if there was one thing he'd learned in his years as a cop, it was that looks could be deceiving.

Just because the blonde looked innocent didn't mean it was true.

When he saw the woman search in her purse and pull out money, he knew that something was indeed going on and realized buying treats for his kids was going to have to wait. Today was his day off, but he was a cop, he always carried, and he wasn't going to walk away from a drug deal just because he wasn't supposed to be working today.

Only as he walked closer, he watched the man grab the woman as she tried to step away from him. The man yanked her up against his body, and while he couldn't see what was happening from this angle, because now both their backs were to him, he'd seen the fear in the woman's face.

Drug deal or mugging?

About to shout out an order for them to freeze, he could get them both in handcuffs and then sort out what was going on once backup arrived, he saw the glint of a knife catch in the sunlight, then press against the woman's neck as they both started moving.

Kidnapping.

Picking up the pace, he darted around a couple of cars, hoping to come out in front of the pair, but they stopped in front of a Porsche, and the woman fumbled in her purse for keys. Knowing this could go really bad, really quickly, Grant pulled out his cell phone, dialed 911, and then dropped his phone on the ground.

The open-ended call would have dispatch sending a patrol car to check things out, but while he waited for backup he was going to have to make his move.

"Going to need you to move the knife from the lady's throat," Grant announced, weapon held in steady hands as he moved in closer to where the man in the hoodie was trying to shove the woman in pink into the driver's seat of her car.

Both of them startled, and when the woman's light blue eyes met his, her mouth dropped open in shock, and his steady hands began to tremble.

Ashlyn Davidson.

No longer a redhead, the light blonde color suited her even better. She was paler than she'd been the night they spent together, and instead of happy with a hint of wistful jealousy, her eyes were now filled with pure, unbridled terror.

"Back up, this doesn't concern you," the man snarled, pressing the blade of his knife deep enough into Ashlyn's neck to draw blood.

The sight of blood on her slender neck had protective rage bubbling up inside him.

He would have done everything within his power to save the woman, no matter who she was, even if she had just participated in a drug deal. But now, knowing it was the woman he'd been unable to get out of his head for three very long months, there was not a chance in hell anything was going to stop him from saving her life.

"Actually, sir, it does. I'm Detective Bull, and I'm going to ask you again to remove the knife from the lady's neck. Set it down on the ground, and get down on your knees, hands in the air."

While he didn't expect the man to comply, he was going to give him a choice before he did something that couldn't be taken back. Like blow the man's head off for daring to lay a finger on Ashlyn.

Panic darted in the ice blue eyes that looked back at him, panic flared in Ashlyn's baby blues as well, but along with that panic was a heavy dose of trust. Knowing that she trusted him to get her out of this alive, had his resolve hardening.

"Last warning, sir," Grant said. Since Ashlyn was much shorter than her assailant, he had a clean shot at the man. Killing him would get him a whole lot of paperwork and an investigation into the use of lethal force, but Grant found he didn't care in the least. So long as Ashlyn walked away today alive, nothing else mattered.

It was going to come to that, he could tell it was.

The man wasn't going to comply, he was going to do something stupid, something that would get Ashlyn killed.

Preparing himself to take the shot, he was unprepared for Ashlyn to suddenly ram her elbow back into the man's ribs.

Her assailant grunted, but the knife dropped from her neck, and she was able to dart away from him, scrambling around her car, while Grant didn't hesitate to throw himself at the man, tackling him to the ground.

Despite his need to get to Ashlyn, confirm she was okay, not bleeding out, he didn't look for her until he'd slapped a pair of handcuffs on the man and kicked the knife well out of reach.

Only then did he look over his shoulder to find Ashlyn cowering against her car.

Dragging her into his arms was the most natural thing in the world.

When her trembling body pressed closer against his, her fingers grabbing fistfuls of his T-shirt, he couldn't help but feel it was fate that had led him here today.

Fate had brought him here to save the life of the woman he'd been obsessing about for months, and who was he to argue with fate?

CHAPTER
Five

May 9th
    4:44 P.M.

This was going to end.

Soon.

And she wasn't ready for it.

Ashlyn hadn't even stopped shaking yet, but she knew that Grant staying with her this long was only because of the night they'd shared. If she was anyone else, he would have already handed her off to another cop, or a paramedic, or even just sent her off home on her own.

Thankfully, he hadn't done any of that, and she was still curled against his side, sitting in the back of his car, holding fistfuls of his T-shirt, and praying that the seconds slowed down a little so she could stay just how she was.

Other than when she'd had to give her statement and Grant had given his, he hadn't left her side. Even then, she knew he hadn't wanted to, but they both needed to give statements, and they couldn't do that together.

Which sucked.

Big time.

Not that the cop who had taken her statement was mean or anything. In fact, the woman had been kind, thoughtful, and genuine, and that had helped a lot. But it didn't make saying the words any easier. Admitting that her would-be kidnapper had been going to make her give him money, jewelry, and then her body.

A shiver wracked through her, and Grant's arm around her tightened.

"I think that's all we need, right?" he asked his colleagues pointedly.

"Yes. If you think of anything else, or you need anything, then don't hesitate to call, Ms. Davidson," the older man told her. "Here's a card for a victims' support group if you feel like it's something that would benefit you."

With a shaking hand, she reached out and took it. She had no idea if she would use it, but it would be rude not to take it. Tucking it into her purse, she went to slide out of Grant's car, and although his grip tightened once again, he then took a deep breath and let her go.

"You want me to call your brother? Your mom?" he asked. When she shook her head, he glanced over at her car. "Want me to follow you to your place?"

"No!" The word burst out of her, and she shook her head vehemently.

"Okay then," he said, looking defeated and disappointed. "You can call if you need anything."

"Wait." Grabbing his arm when he went to move, she held onto him, needing his steady presence. "The no was for driving my car. I don't think ... I can't ... after what ... I don't want the car anymore. I'm going to sell it." It would be a reminder of what had almost happened to her today. What would have happened if Grant hadn't shown up.

"Okay then," he repeated, only this time he sounded much more relaxed. Happier even. "Can I drive you home?"

"Is it too much of a bother?"

"Not a bother at all."

"Then I'd like that." She offered him a shy smile. Unlike at her brother's wedding, she wasn't wearing all her armor so she didn't feel confident. There was blood on her clothes, a bandage on her neck, she was shaky and scared. There was nothing attractive about her right now.

Guiding her into the front seat of his vehicle, once she gave him her address, he programmed it into the GPS, and they rode in a companionable silence. There was so much she wanted to say, questions she wanted to ask, wanted desperately to know if he'd thought about her at all in the last few months and confess he'd been nearly constantly on her mind.

Instead, she said nothing, just fiddled idly with the hem of her sweater, and wished she lived further away so she could spend more time with Grant. The fifteen minutes it took to drive to her place didn't feel like enough, and when he parked out front of her building, she didn't want to leave the safety of his car.

"I can walk you up," he offered, and her gaze snapped to his.

"If it's not a bother."

"Not a bother at all."

His fingers closed around hers as they crossed the street and walked into her building. Her penthouse apartment was beautiful, but felt so lonely lately, and when they climbed out of the elevator she didn't want to let him go.

"Please," she whimpered as she pressed her lips to his. Not really sure what she was even asking for. All Ashlyn knew was that she needed to rid herself of the trauma that had been this afternoon.

"Honey, you were just—"

"Don't care. Want you. Need you. Haven't been able to stop thinking about you." When her hands fumbled with his zipper, he didn't stop her, and when she reached into his boxers and freed his length, it was already growing hard.

She didn't want this sweet and slow, didn't want to make love, just wanted him inside her, filling her up, cleaning away the filth of the day. Shoving down her own jeans and panties, when she grabbed his length again, he growled.

"Tell me you're sure," he ordered.

"Surer than anything else in my life."

At her words, he grabbed her hips and lifted her off the floor. Automatically, her hands grabbed at his shoulders, and her legs wrapped around his waist. Adjusting herself, she took him inside her in one smooth move.

"Condom, Ash," he growled.

"I'm clean and on birth control," she assured him. She got it, he had two kids with a wife he loved and wasn't looking for a baby. Neither was she. Well, at least not under these circumstances.

"I'm clean too," he told her.

"Perfect." Unable to hold back, she began to move her hips, urging him to meet her thrust for thrust.

"Play with yourself, I'm not going to last long," he commanded, and like she was helpless to do anything but obey, one of her hands moved to touch herself where their bodies joined.

She'd never touched herself in front of anyone before, and while she might have been embarrassed, the way Grant watched her chased away those feelings before they could take hold.

The heat in his eyes, her fingers on her bundle of nerves, and him thrusting inside her all combined to have pleasure building quickly. When Grant took her mouth in a hungry kiss that was all it took, and she combusted into a fiery inferno of ecstasy.

He followed her into pleasure, and as she clung to him, Ashlyn realized it was going to be a whole lot harder to walk away this time than it had been last time.

CHAPTER
Six

Holding her like this, buried inside her, her cheeks flushed with her pleasure, Grant knew one thing for certain. He didn't want to let Ashlyn go.

Which meant they needed to talk. If all their night together had meant to her was one night of fun, then he'd walk away with no regrets. If all this moment in the foyer of her penthouse meant was gratefulness and joy at being alive, then he'd walk away with no regrets.

But if she wanted more ...

Please let her want more.

"Thank you," she whispered, her voice muffled because she'd pressed her face against his neck.

"Don't thank me for saving your life, honey," he rebuked gently. He would have saved anyone he'd stumbled across being kidnapped today, it just so happened that it was her, the woman he couldn't get out of his head.

When he went to pull out of her so she could go and clean up, and then they could talk, she tightened her legs around his hips, keeping him deep inside her. It was obvious she was deeply affected, but by them having sex or what could have happened to her?

He'd heard her statement, the man who had held a knife to her throat had planned to rape her once he robbed her. Whether he would have let her go or not afterward they'd never know, but even if she'd lived, Ashlyn would never have been the same. Even now, she'd have scars from her ordeal, and he wasn't talking about the small wound on her neck.

Carrying her through the foyer and into a living room, he sat down on an overstuffed armchair and settled her in his lap. She sighed contentedly and snuggled closer, seemingly pleased to still have him inside her.

"I'm so glad it was you there today," she admitted, her face once again pressed to his neck.

"Me too, honey. Me too." Should he just admit that he hadn't been able to stop thinking about her? Was that appropriate given what she'd been through today? Maybe he should hold on to that particular piece of information until she wasn't so emotionally raw.

Now he had her number, and they'd reconnected today, he could quite easily stay in touch under the guise of checking up on her, and then maybe in a few weeks or months he could broach the topic of dating.

If it wasn't for the almost kidnapping, he'd just be honest with her. Grant had always been the kind of guy who told things like they were, but in the most compassionate way he could, and now that he was in his forties, he had even less interest in beating around the bush. But he also didn't want to overload Ashlyn when she was already vulnerable.

Lifting her head from his shoulder, she chewed on her bottom lip in a way that made it pretty hard to resist running his tongue along it to soothe away the teeth marks. Conflicting emotions raged in her pretty blue eyes, and he had to wonder if she was trying to think about how to let him down gently.

His chest tightened uncomfortably at the thought. Of course, he would never push her into a relationship she didn't want, and if she truly wasn't interested in him, he'd walk away, but he hoped that wasn't the case.

"I can't stop thinking about you."

"I haven't been able to get you out of my head," Ashlyn said at the exact same time.

Both their eyes widened at their simultaneous confessions, and then a huge grin curled his lips into a smile. She did feel the same way he did. Thank goodness, because he was pretty sure he was kidding himself when he thought he could walk away without regrets. There would have been none about sex with Ashlyn, she was beautiful inside and out, but he would have regretted not getting a chance with her.

"Really?" she asked, with just a hint of suspicion. "You're not just saying that because ... of what happened today? If you're not interested, I can take it, you don't have to coddle me or anything. I'm stronger than I look."

"No coddling," he promised. "I swear, Ashlyn, I can't stop thinking about you. I ... kept your panties from that night," he admitted. "I still have them, and they haven't just sat in a drawer these last few months."

At his confession, her cheeks pinked, but she looked pretty pleased at his revelation. "I wanted to ask for your number so many times these last few months, but I know you still love your wife."

"Oh, honey." Lifting his hands to frame her face, he let his fingertips feather gentle caresses on her temples. "I will always love Lara, but she's gone and she's not coming back. She would want me to move on, to try to find someone else to share my life with, and there has been no one before you. You were the first woman to make me think I could actually do that. Actually build a new life."

"Really?"

"Really," he assured her. "This is all new to me. It's been a long time, and last time I dated I didn't come with a couple of kids. But I'm game to explore this thing between us if you are." *Please don't back out now.*

"Your kids ... will they be okay with you dating someone?"

"We've never been in this position, but I like to think I've raised two great kids with open minds who would understand that my dating someone else doesn't mean forgetting about their mom. Not that I would let Lara come between us," Grant quickly added. "Part of my heart will always belong to her, but if we were together, my focus would be on you." Realizing how that sounded, he quickly added, "Not that I'm after declarations of love today. I just meant that if I was with you, I would be with you, I wouldn't try to bring Lara into the mix."

"I knew what you meant," she told him, a warm smile lighting her face. "And I would never ask you to pretend she wasn't a major part of your life and the mother of your kids."

"So," he drew the word out. "We're going to give dating a chance?"

"Depends. Are you asking me out on a date, Detective Bull?" she asked, amusement dancing in her pretty blue eyes.

"Will you have dinner with me, Ms. Davidson?"

CHAPTER
Seven

May 10th
8:56 A.M.

Was she ready to do this?

Ashlyn nervously smoothed her palms down the skirt of her dress as she waited for Grant to answer his front door, wondering if she should have picked something else to wear. Was she dressed too formally? Not formally enough? What were you supposed to wear to meet the kids of the guy you liked?

Really liked.

After he'd asked her out yesterday and she'd accepted, they'd decided that she would meet his kids in the morning, just so that there were no secrets between them. The kids were fifteen and twelve, and she'd asked as many questions as she could about them, so she felt like she had some things she could say and ask about to show she was genuinely interested.

This would be the first time she'd ever dated a guy with kids, and it was Grant's first time dating since his wife died, so she knew they were both nervous about how things were going to go. She hoped to get to know Lindsay and Kevin, alongside getting to know Grant, but she didn't want to put pressure on them. If they wanted to take things slow, that was fine with her.

When the door opened and Grant stood there, Ashlyn felt a little of her anxiety melt away. After all, these kids had been raised by Grant, so she knew they had to be amazing young people.

Of course, she knew that even if they didn't like her, that didn't mean they still weren't great kids. She'd been thrilled when her mom started dating her now stepdad, there had been that instant connection between all of them, and she couldn't deny she was hoping things went as smoothly now for her and Grant.

"Hi." She smiled, stepping into his embrace when he opened his arms.

"Hi," he said back, brushing a chaste kiss to her lips. When he pulled back, his gaze was scrutinizing as he gave her a once-over. "Did you sleep okay? How's your neck?"

"I took some sleeping pills to help me sleep, and I must have been pretty drained because I don't remember budging during the night. No dreams. My neck is sore, but no signs of infection," she assured him. Nightmares were going to come for her at some point, she was pretty sure about that, but at least they had given her last night to get some proper and much-needed rest.

"Good. I didn't like the idea of you being alone all night."

"I promised to call one of my brothers or my mom if I needed to, and you had to come home to your kids," she reminded him. He'd offered to stay with her and ask someone to stay with his kids, but she wanted to make a good impression on them, and taking him away from them when they didn't even know yet that the two of them were dating seemed wrong.

"You ready to meet them?" he asked, guiding her into the house and closing the door behind them.

"As I'll ever be," she replied, dragging in a deep breath, not wanting to admit just how nervous she really was.

"It's going to go fine," he assured her, and she hoped he was right.

They walked down a hall, and she noted a living room on the left, and an office on the right, before they stepped into a large, open, airy, kitchen meals family room space. A large wall of windows ran along the back wall, with a set of French doors that opened onto a deck. The yard looked a good size and was mostly lawn and several large trees. The inside space was modern and clean, and while she had more traditional tastes in furnishings, the room had a homey feel to it that she loved.

Two kids sat at the table. A pretty girl was scrolling her phone, and a lanky preteen boy who glanced over at them.

"Who's that?" the boy asked, making his sister's head snap up.

Wanting to let Grant make the introductions, she offered both kids smiles as Grant led her closer to the table.

"Kevin, Lindsay, this is Ashlyn."

The boy eyed her with curiosity, and she started to let her guard down a little, until she noticed how Lindsay had curled her nose up.

"You guys remember Jessica, with little Freddie from the station. Remember how I went to her wedding a few months back?" Grant continued. "Well, Ashlyn is Jessica's husband's little sister."

"Are you dating her?" Kevin asked.

"Dating?" Lindsay shrieked, shoving her chair back and bounding to her feet. "Have you been dating her for months and didn't even tell us?"

"No," Grant hurried to assure his daughter. "I mean, yes, Kevin, I have asked Ashlyn out on a date, and she said yes, but no, we haven't been dating each other for months. We hadn't seen each other since the wedding until yesterday."

"Your superhero dad saved my life," she told the kids. While Kevin's eyes lit up with interest, Lindsay whirled on her, anger seeping out of every pore of the teen's body.

"Dad doesn't date, he loves my mom," Lindsay snarled.

"Of course, I love your mom, Linds," Grant soothed. "I'll always love your mom. Ashlyn and I talked about it, and she knows that, but your mom is gone, and I like Ashlyn, a lot," Grant said firmly.

"Well, unlike her," Lindsay yelled. "I don't want a new mom."

"Oh, sweetie, no," Ashlyn quickly assured the girl. "I don't want to be your new mom. You had a mom who loved you very much. If things work out with your dad and me, then I just want to be another person in your life who cares about you. I swear I would never try to take your mom's place."

"Good, then get out," Lindsay shrieked.

"Lindsay," Grant rebuked. "We don't talk to people like that, especially someone I've told you is important to me."

"I don't care," Lindsay shot back. "If she won't leave, then I am."

The teenager ran up the stairs, leaving all three of them staring after her. Ashlyn didn't know what to say or do, or what Grant was going to say or do, but when he turned to look at her, she knew.

It was over.

His daughter couldn't accept her.

"Would it be okay if you gave me some time to talk things through with my kids?" he asked her, at least sounding apologetic about it.

"Sure," she said, already knowing how that talk would go. If Lindsay wasn't on board with this, it wasn't happening.

"I'll call you later," Grant promised, but as she turned and headed back the way she'd only just come, Ashlyn knew how that call would go.

CHAPTER
Eight

May 10th
   9:05 A.M.

That was not how this was supposed to go.

Not how he'd expected it to go.

It wasn't like Grant had expected his kids to embrace Ashlyn into their lives with open arms, but he hadn't expected his daughter to be so outright rude and angry at the idea of him dating. He'd thought the kids would take it more like Kevin had, vaguely interested, and allow bonds to form naturally over the next few weeks and months.

Seemed like that wasn't happening.

As Ashlyn disappeared back into the hall, and he heard the front door close behind her a moment later, he felt his heart drop. She was the first woman to spark life back into him, and he wasn't going to let her go without a fight.

If things didn't work out between them, that was that, but he wasn't waving the white flag of defeat before they'd even gotten a chance to get things started. She was a beautiful woman, bright and smart, kind and funny, sweet and caring. He knew she had started up her own line of jewelry, which she sold to the rich and famous, and was also active in several charities run by her stepfather's family. She'd wanted to make a good impression on his kids today, and he was angry with his daughter for not even giving her a chance, even as he understood there must be a mess of emotions tangled inside Lindsay right now.

Maybe he should have prepared the kids on his own.

Since this was his first time dating since Lara died, he didn't know the best way to handle things. It looked like some trial and error was going to happen. There was no going back now, he couldn't reintroduce Ashlyn to his kids, and he had to hope his daughter was mature enough to understand that moving on didn't mean forgetting the past.

"I thought she seemed cool," Kevin said from the table, making him smile.

"She is, Kev. She's a nice woman and ..."

"You want it to work out with her?"

"I do. But I also don't want you guys to suffer."

The conflicting emotions inside had him feeling nauseous. How was he supposed to handle this? He was an adult, the dad, and he deserved to have a life, date, fall in love, and be happy, after all, his kids weren't going to be kids forever. On the other hand, they *were* still kids, and his responsibility was to them and raising them.

"Let's go talk to your sister, yeah?"

Kevin nodded and followed him up the stairs. Lindsay's door was closed, and Grant knocked on it, waiting until she okayed it before opening it. While this was his house and his rules, and his kids knew that privacy was a privilege not a right, he tried to be respectful of them wherever possible.

"Good, she's gone," Lindsay said with a smug smile when she opened the door and saw it was just him and her brother standing there.

"I asked her to give me some time to talk to you guys, but I am calling her later, and I will be taking her out on a date," he told his daughter. As much as he loved his kids, they were the only thing that kept him getting out of bed when it felt like grief was going to crush him, he couldn't allow them to think they ran his life.

"Dad!" Lindsay growled. "We don't need her."

"Maybe we don't need her, but I'd like to have her be part of my life, part of all of our lives."

"Why?" Lindsay demanded. "It's just been the three of us since mom died, we don't have to change that."

"Life is full of changes, Linds. It doesn't always turn out the way we think it's going to, the way we plan it out. You guys are getting older. In just a couple of years, you're going to be heading off to college, Kev won't be far behind."

"You get lonely, Dad?" Kevin asked.

"Sometimes," he answered honestly. Before he met Ashlyn, it had been easy to sweep the feelings away in a sea of busyness. But since the wedding, it was getting harder and harder to do that.

"And you're not going to like marry her right now, right?" Kevin asked.

"No, son. Nothing like that. Ashlyn and I would just like to get to know one another and see what happens, but nothing that drastic is happening that quickly."

"I don't want it to happen at all," Lindsay said with a pout.

Kevin shrugged. "I don't care if you date her."

"Kevin!" Lindsay snarled. "You're supposed to be on my side. We don't need a new mommy."

"She said she didn't want to be our mom, just our friend," Kevin said.

"That's what she says now. But what happens when she gets her claws into Dad? Things will change. She'll make us throw away all our photos of Mom, all of Mom's things. She'll want the house to be hers, her rules, her stuff, her decisions. She'll make Dad choose her over us. And what happens when they have a baby? That baby will get all the love and attention, and we'll just be ignored."

"Whoa, Linds," he soothed. "That's a lot of worries about stuff that isn't happening any time soon. If or when Ashlyn and I get married, she would never expect us to get rid of photos of your mom, or special things of hers you guys have. She'd never take over and try to get me to choose her over you. And there are no new babies on the horizon."

"How do you know, Dad? You said you only met her at Jessica's wedding and then again yesterday. You don't really know her at all. How do you know she won't do all the things I just said?" Lindsay asked, arching a brow at him as though she'd just scored several points as she dared him to disagree.

Problem was he couldn't.

His daughter was right. He didn't know Ashlyn very well, and he was running on nothing but instincts.

CHAPTER
Nine

May 10th
10:39 A.M.

It was weird because she hadn't known Grant long, but she felt a gaping hole in her chest where he was supposed to be.

Romantic that she was, Ashlyn had already started to dream about what their future would look like. They'd go out on romantic dates, fall in love with each other one date at a time, his kids would get to know her, like her, accept her as another person in their lives who cared about them, and they'd all become one big happy family.

Only they'd never even crossed the start line, let alone gotten to the finish.

When her elevator dinged to let her know someone was coming up, Ashlyn couldn't even be bothered to drag herself out of her chair to see who it was. Only her parents and brothers had the code to get up to her penthouse, so it wasn't like she needed to worry about some guy with a knife getting into her secure home.

"I don't like finding out that you were attacked through the grapevine at my wife's work, Ashlyn," Donovan's booming voice called out a moment later as he and Jessica came striding into the living room.

"Sorry," she whispered, unable to muster up much enthusiasm for the apology when it felt like her dreams had just been shattered.

Her big brother's gaze zeroed in on the bandage on her neck, and she saw fear flutter through his eyes as he stormed over to her and dragged her off the armchair she'd sat in with Grant less than twenty-four hours ago, and into his arms. A small sob came out as she leaned into her brother's embrace, and she knew she should explain to him that it had nothing to do with the attack and everything to do with the man who had saved her life.

"You okay?" Donovan asked, his voice a little gentler now.

"It's not that." She wept, unable to stop the tears now they'd broken free.

"Then what's wrong?" he asked, thoroughly confused.

"It's Grant ... the wedding ... we ... one night ... couldn't stop thinking ... yesterday ... the knife ... he showed up ... we talked ... we both agreed ... only his kids ... it didn't work out ... I know I shouldn't be this upset but ... felt like it could have been the real thing," she said through her tears, aware she was making little to no sense.

"Didn't get a word of that, Ash," Donovan said, a little amusement coming through his concern.

"Why don't you sit down and tell us, or just your brother, I can go," Jessica offered, but Ashlyn shook her head.

"You can stay," she said, rubbing her fingers at her temples where a headache was brewing.

"Sit. I'm making you tea and getting you some painkillers, then you can explain to us what that rambled monologue actually meant," Donovan teased, making her crack a small smile.

Sinking back down into the armchair, Ashlyn took the blanket Jessica grabbed from the back of the couch and tucked it around herself. By the time Donovan returned with the tea and pills, she'd managed to get her tears under control.

"At your wedding, Grant Bull and I hooked up," she told them. Before now, she'd always kept that one-night stand to herself. Not because she was embarrassed, but because it felt special and she hadn't wanted to share it with anyone.

"You did?" Jessica asked, looking surprised.

"Did he hurt you?" Donovan growled, making her smile again.

"No, at least not how you mean. It was meant to be one night, but I couldn't get him out of my head. Then yesterday he showed up, saved my life, and brought me home afterward. I thought it would never happen because he's a widower with two kids, I didn't think he was looking for anything, but it turns out he couldn't stop thinking about me either," she explained.

"So what's wrong?" Donovan asked.

"His daughter hates me. We wanted to be honest from the beginning, let them know we were dating, so I could get to know them as well. Grant said that's how he wanted to do things, and they're his kids, so I agreed. I went over this morning to meet them, and Kevin seemed okay with it, I think, but Lindsay wasn't."

"She probably just needs time," Jessica said.

"I don't think so. She was pretty adamant she didn't want me to date her dad, and well, he's her dad. Grant has to pick her over me. I mean, I want it to be that way. If mom had made us feel like she was choosing a man over us, we would have hated it. Grant is a good dad, and I want him to be one. I just wish it wasn't a choice. That he could have us both."

Her experience with life and her mom's dating was vastly different than Lindsay's. The teen's mom had died, she wasn't a deadbeat, like Ashlyn's biological father was. When her mom started dating her boss, their entire lives had changed for the better, maybe that had been why it was so easy to accept him into her life.

"Did he tell you that was what he was doing?" Donovan asked. "Choosing his kids over you?"

Ashlyn shook her head. "No, he just asked for time to talk to them, said he'd call me. But what other choice is he going to make? Of course, he has to choose his kids. I mean, they're his kids, and he's the only parent they have left."

The thing was, she really didn't want there to be a choice. She wanted Grant to keep being the amazing dad he was to Lindsay and

Kevin and also date her. She would never try to take those kids' mother's place. That relationship was special, sacred. But she could still be part of their lives, part of their family, and love them in a different way.

When he picked his kids over her, she wouldn't even be angry about it, after all, she wouldn't respect him if he didn't put his responsibilities to his kids as his number one priority. Ashlyn would just be sad as her dreams of what could have been went up in smoke.

CHAPTER
Ten

May 10th
1:17 P.M.

It had been a long day, and it wasn't even half over yet.

Since it was still lunch time, Grant had decided to pick up some takeaway and bring it to Ashlyn's place along with some flowers he hoped would go enough of a way toward getting her to forgive him.

Now he had no idea if he'd handled things the right way. Maybe he should have waited until he and Ashlyn had been dating for a while before telling his kids. Then again, Lindsay had seemed furious at the idea that he might have been keeping a relationship from her, so he doubted that would have changed the outcome of the morning.

Second-guessing himself wasn't going to change anything. He'd done what he thought was the best thing for him, Ashlyn, and his kids, and now he had to make the most of it and work with what he had.

Which, granted, wasn't much.

At least with Lindsay. Kevin seemed okay with the whole thing. He'd been even more intrigued when Grant had told them more about

Ashlyn, the kind of person she was, what she did for a living, and that she drove a Porsche. His car-obsessed kid had been excited after the revelation, and Kevin had asked if, since Ashlyn was rich, did she know any professional race car drivers. He'd told his son he didn't know, but that Kevin could ask her next time he saw her.

Lindsay had made a snarky remark about how she didn't realize they were doing badly financially since he was now after women for their money. Not wanting to lose his cool with his daughter, Grant decided that they all needed a time-out. His former brother-in-law had come over to hang with the kids so he could get out for a bit. Given the high emotional state Lindsay was in, he hadn't wanted her alone while he went to check on Ashlyn.

Thankfully, his cop badge had gotten him into the elevator, and he hadn't corrected the doorman that his visit was to do with yesterday's incident, although he was sure the flowers had given the man doubts.

The question was, were the flowers and lunch enough to get him off the elevator and into Ashlyn's penthouse?

"Oh." The smile fell off Ashlyn's lips when she saw him step out of the elevator. "I thought it was Donovan and Jessica."

"Sorry," he said, feeling awkward with her for the first time.

That was the thing. From the moment he first laid eyes on her, everything had just felt so natural. It was hard to explain. There had been a sense of familiarity even though they hadn't met before. They'd laughed and talked, danced, and when he'd asked if she wanted to find a hotel room, she'd quickly said yes.

Now things felt weird.

Stilted.

Wrong.

"It's okay, I understand." Tears swam in Ashlyn's eyes, and he realized what she thought he meant.

"No," he blurted out, hurrying forward and shoving the flowers into her arms, willing her to understand. "I'm not breaking up with you, I'm not ending things, not that they really got started, but I still want to go out with you. If you'll still have me."

The whole time he'd been talking to his kids, trying to get Lindsay to articulate why it was she was so adamantly against him dating, he'd been aware of the fact that Ashlyn might have decided he was more trouble than he was worth. After all, she was a beautiful, intelligent, funny, kind woman. Any guy would be lucky to have her. He and his kids certainly would.

"You're not ... but Lindsay ... I just assumed you didn't want to go out with me anymore," she finished with a shrug that tried to look nonchalant and failed.

"I was worried you wouldn't want to still go out with me because of Lindsay," he admitted.

"Of course not. She's your daughter, I would never expect you to choose me over her, I don't even want you to have to choose. I never wanted to cause trouble between you and your daughter."

"You're not doing anything," he assured her. "Lindsay ... I don't even know where she's coming from. She seems so angry, so unlike my daughter. She needs some time."

"That's what Jessica said. Donovan agreed with her, of course." Ashlyn rolled her eyes, but she had that wistful look back on her face, the one he recognized from the wedding. She was happy for her brother and his new wife, but she wanted that same kind of love.

Right now, Grant had no way to know if the two of them were going to fall in love, but he wanted the chance to find out. This thing between them felt special, and it deserved a chance to grow.

"I explained to her that while I love her and her brother with every fiber of my being, she won't be dictating my dating life. I assured her that we would be taking things slow, and that you had no intention of taking over the role her mom had. I told her that this was still happening and that she needed to find a way to make peace with it. If she can't talk to me about what's going on, then she can talk to a family member or a therapist. I owe you an apology. I honestly had no idea Lindsay would react that way. If I did, I might have handled things differently."

"You don't need to apologize to me for your daughter being upset." Ashlyn took a step closer, until the bouquet of flowers was all that stopped their bodies from touching.

"Will you go out for dinner with me tomorrow night?" he asked.

"I would love to."

"Can I kiss you now?"

Ashlyn laughed and moved the bouquet to the side so she could step into his arms when he opened them. "You'd better."

CHAPTER
Eleven

August 18th
   11:50 A.M.

Taking a deep breath, she climbed out of her car.

This wasn't going to go well.

It never did.

Ashlyn had been dating Grant for three months now, and if they'd been hoping things would magically improve with his daughter's attitude, they would have been sorely mistaken.

Thankfully, they hadn't expected a magic turnaround. Lindsay had put her foot down and made it abundantly clear that she would not accept her father in a relationship with anyone.

For the last three months, Ashlyn had done her best not to take it personally, only because she was ninety-nine percent sure that Lindsay would have hated anyone Grant brought home and not just her specifically.

Still made it hard though.

She was trying. Doing her best to show both kids that she didn't want to be their new mom, they had a mom, and she didn't want to replace Lara, but Lindsay didn't care. She just hated her. That hatred hadn't dimmed even a little bit, and some days when they did something all four of them together, Ashlyn had to try really hard not to lose control of her emotions.

While she'd never yell at the girl, she definitely might cry, and she knew Lindsay would find a way to try to use that against her.

But Grant was worth fighting for, worth going through all this turmoil because Ashlyn refused to believe that Lindsay would hate her forever. She just had to prove herself. Thank goodness things with Kevin had been easy from the start.

Using his love of all things car-related to her advantage, she was building a strong bond. She'd even wound up keeping the Porsche from the attempted abduction that she'd intended to sell because the twelve-year-old had been so excited about it. It had taken a large amount of self-control not to blurt out that she'd buy him one when he graduated college—then he'd be a little more mature than if she got it when he got his license—but she didn't want to buy Grant's kids love, she wanted to earn it.

She'd still buy him the car, though, she would just surprise him with it. Being a millionaire in her own right with her jewelry brand made her proud. She wasn't just living off the trust fund from her billionaire stepdad or taking handouts. She worked hard for everything she'd earned, but his money, name, influence, and connections had definitely helped.

Carrying the picnic basket she'd painstakingly packed with all of Lindsay and Kevin's favorites, Grant's, too, she headed down to the boat. It was a gorgeous summer's day, and Grant had invited her to join him and the kids out on the ocean.

Of course, she'd said yes. While she treasured their alone time dates, where they got to know each other without the pressure of the kids weighing them down, she enjoyed these family get-togethers, too. Well, at least she enjoyed time with Kevin, and she hoped each time that Lindsay might ease up on her a little.

"Why is *she* here?" Lindsay snarled the second Ashlyn reached the boat.

Guess today is going to be another bad day.

Hang in there, don't give up, Grant is more than worth it.

Since that was absolutely true, she forced her lips up into a smile. "Morning, Lindsay. I made some of those strawberry cinnamon scrolls that you like." Actually, she'd been up half the night looking up recipes and baking them from scratch. She was trying so hard to win over Lindsay, and it was disheartening that she failed every time.

"Yuck. I hate strawberries," Lindsay snapped, even though Ashlyn knew that absolutely wasn't true. Grant said they'd been her favorite fruit since she was a baby.

"Linds," Grant rebuked, coming up behind his daughter and giving her a disapproving frown. "Don't lie. And where are your manners? I raised you better than this. Morning, honey, you look gorgeous." Grant gave her one of those panty-melting smiles of his, and Ashlyn shook off the tension and smiled back.

"I missed you," she admitted as she took his offered hand and stepped onto the boat.

"Missed you too." He leaned in and brushed a chaste kiss to her lips. While they never held back from showing affection in front of his kids, they never took things too far. A soft kiss, holding hands, that was about as far as things went, but they both wanted Lindsay and Kevin to know that they were serious about their relationship.

"You look pretty gorgeous yourself," she told Grant. His shorts cut off just above the knee, showing off his muscled calves, and the T-shirt he was wearing did little to hide his chiseled abs and bulging biceps since the material was all but molded to him.

"Ash." Kevin's eyes lit up when he spotted her, and when he came over and held out his fist, she didn't hesitate to bump it with her own.

"There might be some homemade caramel chocolate chip cookies in here," she told the boy as she held up the picnic basket. "I made the caramel myself, then cut it up and put it in with the chocolate chips."

"Cool. Can I have some now, or do I have to wait until after lunch?"

When he directed the question to her instead of his father, Ashlyn immediately looked to Grant. She never wanted to interfere with his parenting. If they wound up married—and honestly, she wanted that more with each passing date—then she would back up his rules, but she didn't want to step in where she wasn't supposed to be.

Grant said nothing, just gave her an encouraging nod, and she refocused on Kevin. "Today is about having fun, so eat the cookies now. But maybe leave at least a couple for the rest of us."

The boy grinned and reached out to take the basket. "Maybe," he teased as he wandered off to eat his cookies.

As she watched him, Ashlyn felt her heart swell with joy. Lindsay might still hate her, but she was making more progress with Kevin every time they hung out together. She really liked the kid, and she was sure she'd like Lindsay, too, if the teen would just allow her to get to know her.

Although Ashlyn was starting to feel like that was nothing more than wishful thinking.

CHAPTER
Twelve

August 18th
3:37 P.M.

He'd never been disappointed in either of his kids before now.

Of course, over the years, Grant had gotten annoyed with them, he was only human, and so were they, and there had been plenty of times they'd been naughty. When they'd been pregnant with Lindsay, he and Lara had discussed how they wanted to parent, and they both agreed that rules and routines were good for kids, but so was the ability to speak freely about their thoughts and feelings. Mom and Dad weren't always going to be there, and they wanted their kids to feel independent enough to be able to acknowledge whatever they were feeling and then think through the consequences of any decisions they wanted to make.

Over the years, that had worked well for him. His kids learned early on to come to him and speak freely without judgment. It didn't mean that he sometimes didn't have to enact consequences for poor choices, but he thought he had his kids' trust.

Turned out he'd been very wrong on that.

Despite over three months having passed since he announced he and

Ashlyn were dating, Lindsay hadn't softened her stance even a little bit. He hadn't been expecting his kids to jump all in enthusiastically to the idea, but he hadn't expected this either.

Neither he nor Ashlyn expected Lindsay to look at her as a mother figure, and they were both prepared to ease the kids into the idea of them dating, but Lindsay was being completely unreasonable, and despite him giving her multiple chances to explain what was bothering her, she refused to talk.

"Hey," he rebuked as he caught a glimpse of Lindsay tossing the homemade strawberry cinnamon scrolls Ashlyn had made her completely from scratch over the side of the boat.

"Oh, oops," Lindsay said with what could only be described as a mean smile on her face.

When had his daughter learned to be mean? She could dislike the idea of him dating someone without needing to be cruel about it, and some of the things he'd caught her doing and saying to Ashlyn could only be described as cruel.

Where had his sweet, kind, compassionate daughter gone?

It was like in the blink of an eye, she had turned into someone he didn't even recognize.

"Accident," Lindsay added with a sneer. While he'd hoped Ashlyn hadn't noticed since she was deep in conversation with Kevin, when Lindsay looked past him to where the pair were talking and smirked, he knew his girlfriend had indeed seen what his daughter had done.

That was it. He'd had enough of his daughter's attitude. It was time for her to either tell him what was going on inside her head so he knew how to help her, or start treating Ashlyn with respect.

"Inside, now," he snapped at Lindsay in the rare, angry father voice his kids had never given him much cause to bring out.

Eyes widening at his tone, Lindsay tried batting her eyelashes at him and giving him her I'm just your cute little daughter look, but he wasn't having it. When she realized that, she gave an annoyed huff and stood, sauntering her way into the boat's small cabin.

Taking a seat at the little table in there, Grant waited until his daughter sat opposite him, and then he studied her, trying to figure out what had changed Lindsay into this girl he didn't even recognize.

"What's going on?" he asked. They'd had this conversation several times over, but he was yet to get any sort of answer.

"Nothing."

"Don't lie to me. We don't do that in this family."

"You lied about *her*," Lindsay seethed.

"I absolutely did not. I met her one time at a wedding, then again the day before we told you about us. I didn't want to lie, that's why I told you and your brother from the beginning." He still wasn't sure whether he'd made the right move, but it was what it was.

"We don't need her."

"It's not about need. I *want* Ashlyn in my life."

"Well, I don't."

"I'm sorry to hear that, Lindsay, because she's going to be part of your life." Grant loved his kids with his entire being, but he was falling in love with Ashlyn, and he refused to let his teenage daughter bully him into breaking off the relationship.

"She's always hanging around. Butting into our family things," Lindsay said with a pout.

"That's categorically untrue. I go out on a date with her once a week, and this is maybe the sixth time she's done something with all of us together. We've gone out on the boat at least half a dozen times this summer, and this is the first time she's joined us." He was doing his best to balance both parts of his life and make sure everyone was getting the attention they deserved.

"I don't want her around at all. Ever. I hate her." Lindsay said it with such conviction that Grant feared his daughter meant it. He had no idea what that meant for his future relationship with Ashlyn, or with Lindsay. But he did know he wasn't giving up on either of them.

"If you won't speak to me, tell me why you're so adamantly against me dating Ashlyn, then I think I'm going to book you an appointment with a therapist. Maybe that will help. But make no mistake about it, I love you more than you will ever know, but I will not tolerate this bad behavior any longer. You will start treating Ashlyn with the same respect that she shows you. Starting with an apology for throwing the strawberry cinnamon scrolls she made for you overboard."

"No," Lindsay said simply, shoving to her feet. "I'm not a little kid anymore, I'm going to be sixteen in less than six months. I'm not apologizing to her for anything. She should be apologizing to me."

With that, his daughter stormed off back outside, down the opposite end of the deck from where Kevin and Ashlyn were still talking, leaving Grant staring after her, wondering how he was ever going to join all the pieces of his life together to make one where everybody was happy.

CHAPTER
Thirteen

December 1st
  6:11 P.M.

Drawing in a deep breath, Ashlyn gave herself a few seconds to pull herself together.

This had become her custom over the last several months whenever she was going to be spending time with Grant and his kids.

It was getting increasingly difficult to deal with this.

Despite the fact that it had been almost seven months since Grant saved her life and asked her out, Lindsay hadn't budged one tiny little bit. In fact, things had gotten much worse, although she hadn't told Grant about it.

Somehow, Lindsay had gotten hold of Ashlyn's number and was constantly blowing up her phone with a barrage of nasty messages. Since she was quite literally a millionaire in her own right, the teenager couldn't call her a gold digger, so instead Lindsay had been calling her a whore, saying she was selling her rich self to Grant for time and attention.

While of course she knew none of that was true, the language the girl used, the venom in her tone, the pure hatred, it was wearing her down, making her wonder if maybe this was just never going to work out.

Seven months and no changes.

How much longer were they supposed to give things?

Grant had Lindsay in therapy since the day on the boat last summer when Lindsay had thrown overboard the homemade treats Ashlyn had painstakingly made for her. It didn't seem to help. Instead of getting less angry and more used to the idea of her dad dating, Lindsay was just doubling down and getting more and more furious.

The last thing Ashlyn wanted was for Grant to lose his daughter because of her.

Over the last couple of months, the teenager's anger bled over toward her dad and her brother, and Ashlyn had found herself praying for a Christmas miracle. Walking away from Grant would be heartbreaking. She already loved him, but she was feeling more selfish by the day, no matter how many times Grant apologized for his daughter's behavior and asked her not to give up on them yet.

She didn't want to, but this was slowly killing all of them, and it already felt like things were hopeless.

"Christmas miracle needed desperately," she murmured to the universe as she walked up the path to Grant's front door.

It was obvious he'd known she was out there, because the door opened as soon as she was on the porch, before she even had a chance to ring the bell.

"Sorry," she said immediately, not knowing if he'd seen her just standing out there.

"Don't apologize, honey," he said, drawing her into his arms. "I'm the one who should be apologizing. I'm so sorry things haven't improved. I hate that you're hurting."

"It's not your fault," she assured him, pressing her face to his neck and breathing in his comforting woodsy scent.

"Since I'm the one who raised Lindsay, I can pretty much say it is."

Hating the recrimination in his tone, she nuzzled his neck and then lifted her head so she could meet his gaze. "It's not. This is just hard, and—"

Touching a finger to her lips, he silenced her, the pain in his eyes making her chest ache. "No ands. Please," he begged.

"We have to accept—"

"We don't."

"I don't want you to lose your daughter."

"I don't want to lose either of you."

Ashlyn could see that was true, and even though they were yet to exchange I love yous she could see that he loved her. That knowledge buoyed her a little, and she offered him the biggest smile she could muster. "We can hang in there a little longer."

"Thank you, I know how hard this is for you." Pulling her in for a quick kiss, he took her hand and guided her down to the family room.

"You guys have been busy," she said when she saw that their tree was up, it had lights on it, and there were boxes of decorations sitting open, stacked around it.

"I would have asked you to join us to decorate, but doing the tree was something Lindsay used to love doing with her mom, and now the three of us do it together every year. Given how things are, I thought it might be better to stick with that this year."

"You don't have to explain, that's fine," she rushed to assure him. The last thing she wanted was for any of the three of them to feel she was forcing her way in where she wasn't wanted.

"Wasn't going to leave you out of this tradition, though," he said, giving her a somewhat forced smile as he went to the kitchen counter and picked up a basket. It was red and white checked, with little felt Christmas trees, Santa hats, holly, and Santas circling it.

"That's adorable, what is it?"

"Every year we do a special Christmas advent, each day in December, we don't just eat a piece of chocolate, we do something Christmassy. I thought maybe the kids would have grown out of it by now. Linday is almost sixteen and Kevin just turned thirteen last month, but they still said they wanted to do it."

"Aww, that's so sweet."

"Day one is choosing our secret Santas."

Hearing that had her heart dropping. There was no way this was going to work out. Lindsay wouldn't want her to be part of this.

"Grant—"

"We're doing it," he said, cutting her off, voice fierce. "Kids, come downstairs, please."

"She's not going to—"

"She has to accept that this is happening. I love my daughter, and I'm falling for you, I have been taking things slow, but I won't let her have the power to dictate to me who can be in my life and who can't."

Ashlyn nodded, but her stomach cramped when she heard footsteps on the stairs. Then plummeted further when the kids came into view, and Lindsay's smile dropped, replaced by a sneer, when the girl saw her.

"Time to pick our secret Santas," Grant said, voice forced with cheerfulness.

"Dad, she's not doing it with us," Lindsay immediately protested.

"Don't test me on this, Linds," Grant told his daughter, managing to keep his voice calm but firm.

"I don't care if Ashlyn joins in," Kevin piped up, and both she and Grant shot the boy grateful smiles.

"Because you're a traitor to mom. You both are," Lindsay screeched, but her father simply held up the basket she presumed had all their names on bits of paper inside.

"You can go first, Lindsay."

There must have been a note in her father's voice that said he wasn't compromising, because Lindsay huffed, but stomped over and angrily snatched her bit of paper.

"You're next, honey." Grant held the basket in front of her, and Ashlyn summoned a smile as she reached in and took her piece of paper.

Kevin went next, followed by Grant. Then he set the basket back down on the kitchen counter and included them all in his smile.

"Rules are you can't spend more than ten dollars, the gift has to be something thoughtful, not generic like candy. And we exchange the gifts on Christmas Eve," Grant explained for her benefit. "Everyone, unfold your paper and see who you got."

With trembling fingers, Ashlyn unfolded hers, dread clogging her throat when she saw the name printed there.

Lindsay.

Because that wasn't going to end in disaster.

CHAPTER

Fourteen

December 3rd
   5:42 P.M.

This was probably a bad idea, but Grant wasn't backing down.

Lindsay had to understand that she wasn't going to rule their family. He respected his kids, valued their opinions, but they didn't dictate who he got to date. He was falling in love with Ashlyn, and he knew she was floundering, feeling like giving up on their relationship was the only way to bring peace to his family.

But it wasn't.

If his daughter cost him this second chance at love, something he'd never thought he would find again, then he worried he would always subconsciously hold that against her.

In the last seven months, Lindsay still hadn't been able to articulate to him why she was so against him dating. He got it was an adjustment, the kids were used to his attention being focused on them, but it wasn't like he'd thrown them to the wind and was focused only on Ashlyn. Between his work and hers, the kids' school and extracurricular activities, he didn't spend anywhere near as much time with Ashlyn as he wanted to.

"Dad, Ash is here, in her Porsche. Can I go sit in it for a bit?" Kevin called from the front of the house, and he smiled. His son was really bonding with Ashlyn, and he loved seeing the two become more comfortable with each other.

"Sure thing, Kev," he called back. Once the front door closed behind his son, he took a deep, calming breath, and called his daughter. "Linds, time to come down."

Silence met his call, and then a minute later, stomping.

Lindsay was pouting like a toddler when she came down the stairs. Grant had always considered his daughter fairly mature, and it hurt to know not only was he wrong about that, but that she wouldn't open up to him. It wasn't like Ashlyn had ever done anything to hurt Lindsay, yet his daughter's anger ran so deep.

"Is *she* coming?" Lindsay snarled.

"You know she is. I told you she was going to do our Advent calendar tradition with us this year. She did the secret Santa pick, and did Christmas karaoke with us yesterday, of course she's coming today. Kevin went out to look at her car, then they'll be coming in."

More stomping as he went to the kitchen table to ensure he hadn't forgotten anything, and Lindsay followed. "That's not fair. You get to bring your girlfriend, but you wouldn't let me bring my boyfriend."

"You know the rules, you're allowed one date a week, and you already had your date with Everett this week. Plus, this is a family thing."

"Then why is *she* here. She's not family and she's never going to be."

Sighing, Grant reached over and grabbed his daughter, dragging her in for a quick hug even though she didn't return it. "Nothing is ever going to stop me from loving you, that's the way real love works, it's forever. In the same way I'll never stop loving your mom, and neither will you or your brother. Ashlyn isn't asking any of us not to love your mom. The heart is a pretty big organ, it can fit a whole lot of love inside it. Loving Ashlyn doesn't take away any of the love we have for your mom. That's not the way love is. I can love your mom and love Ashlyn all at the same time."

"Do you love her?" Lindsay demanded.

The front door banged open, and he heard Ashlyn and Kevin giggling together as they came down the hall. The answer to his daughter's question was a simple one.

"Yeah," he whispered, "I do."

"Hey." Ashlyn's eyes lit up as she stepped into the room and saw him, and he quickly crossed to her, pulling her into a hug and dropping a kiss to her lips.

"Hey, yourself."

"Thanks for inviting me." Ashlyn's gaze darted somewhat nervously to where he'd left Lindsay, and he had no doubt his daughter's expression was hostile.

"Told you you were being part of the Bull family Christmas Advent spectacular," he teased.

"What are we doing today?" Ashlyn asked.

"Gingerbread house building and decorating competition," Kevin piped up before he could answer.

"Ooh, fun! Since my mom always loved baking, we used to make a gingerbread house together every year. At the time, I never thought much about it, I was too young, but now I realize she had to scrimp and scrounge every penny she could to do that for us. After she married my stepdad, we kept the tradition going. Decorating the house with my mom and brothers, they're some of my happiest Christmas memories."

"Let's see if we can add to those memories," Grant said, touching a kiss to Ashlyn's temple and then guiding her to the table.

"Who does the judging?" Ashlyn asked as he pulled her chair out for her and then took the seat beside her. He'd set up the parts of the house in front of each seat, and then the middle of the table was filled with all the things they could use to decorate.

"Grandma and Grandpa, and Nanny and Poppy," Kevin answered. "We take pictures and send them to them without names attached, then they each give a vote on the winner."

"So you don't need to worry about winning," Lindsay snarked. "I'm going to tell them which one is yours so they don't pick it."

Ashlyn's smile dropped a bit, but Kevin rolled his eyes at his sister.

"Her mom owns Eat Dessert First, as if she's not going to be better at this than all of us," Kevin said, making Ashlyn laugh and relax a little, and Grant sent up a silent prayer of thanks that his son wasn't having the same problems with Ashlyn as Lindsay was.

"I think you might be disappointed then, Kev, because I'm nowhere near as good at baking as my mom is."

"Nah." Kevin shook his head in disagreement. "Everything you've ever baked for me has been amazing. You're going to win."

Determined not to let Lindsay and her terrible attitude ruin a fun evening, Grant got to work building his gingerbread house, and the others all followed suit. He, Ashlyn, and Kevin chatted and laughed, Lindsay didn't join in, but at least she was sulking silently as she built her house.

He'd hoped that spending these joyful Christmassy moments together might help Lindsay relax and overcome her anger, but it didn't seem to be working.

Was he hoping for something that was never going to happen?

And if he was, where did that leave him?

Walking away from his daughter was obviously not on the table, but walking away from Ashlyn felt impossible as well.

CHAPTER
Fifteen

December 3rd
10:58 P.M.

"It's late. I really should get going," Ashlyn announced, glancing at the time on her phone. But she made no attempt to move out of Grant's embrace.

They were snuggled side by side on his couch, watching old Christmas movies, and while she knew she had to get up and go home at some point, she found herself really not wanting to. Despite Lindsay's hostile behavior, it had been a fun evening. Making gingerbread houses had been nostalgic in the best way, and she, Kevin, and Grant had laughed and talked and gushed over each other's houses, although after her first few compliments of Lindsay's creation were met with anger, Ashlyn had backed off and just let the teen be.

The kids had gone up to their rooms once they'd taken the photos and sent them off to the grandparents for judging. Well, they'd sent off Grant's and the kids', Ashlyn had insisted that hers not be in the running to win, saying she was happy enough to just be included. Which was absolutely true.

"Mmm." Grant nuzzled her neck, the arm that was draped over her shoulders pulling her closer against him. "I don't want to let you go yet."

"Don't want to go either," she told him, tilting her head to the side to give him better access to her neck. Hopefully, one day they could share moments like this every night, but that felt so far away, almost like it was forever moving further into the distance.

"Then stay."

Jerking her head up in surprise, Ashlyn met Grant's gaze, half expecting to find he was just joking.

Only he didn't look like he was joking.

In fact, he looked like he was deadly serious.

"I ... c-can't," she stammered.

"Why?"

"Your kids. Well daughter. Lindsay would freak if she found out I spent the night, and I don't want to have to sneak out of here before dawn like some dirty little secret." While she wanted to be respectful to Grant's daughter and his relationship with his child, she didn't want to lose respect for herself in the process. And sneaking out of the house would definitely make her feel that way.

A growl rumbled through Grant, and his brows snapped together to form a V as he dragged her into his lap. "Never suggested you should sneak out, honey."

"If I don't, then Lindsay will know I slept over."

"Then she'll know."

"She hates me."

"It's been seven months since we started dating. I've given her time to get used to the idea. I want to spend the night with you in my arms. Stay. Please."

Searching his dark eyes to confirm he was telling her the truth, when she saw nothing in them but honesty, Ashlyn slowly nodded. This was probably going to be a bad idea, but if Grant was sure, then she would stay.

"Okay," she agreed.

His face broke out into one of those panty-melting, heart-shattering smiles, and Ashlyn looped her arms around his neck and squeaked when he scooped her up and darted toward the stairs. Giggling as he carried her up, she did her best not to grind against him, something which was pretty difficult since the bulge in his pants was currently pressed snugly against her center, because she didn't want one of the kids to come out of their rooms and catch them.

"Relax, they're asleep," Grant murmured in her ear. Then his lips found the pulse point on her neck and sucked hard enough to make her moan.

Inside his bedroom, Grant set her on her feet. As he went about undressing her, pausing to touch soft kisses and gentle caresses to her skin, staring at her with such tender affection, Ashlyn felt her heart swell in her chest, and the words came bursting out of her.

"I love you." As she said them, she froze. While they were true, she hadn't really meant to say them yet. She was almost positive Grant loved her back, but his first loyalty was to his kids, and she was pretty sure that she and Lindsay were never going to manage a relationship. "Sorry," she quickly added, not wanting him to feel like she was pressuring him for more than he was able to give her right now.

Another growl rumbled through his chest. "Did you mean it?"

Ashlyn nodded. She wouldn't lie about something like that.

"Are you taking it back?"

"Yes. No. I'm not ... I don't know," she finished lamely.

"Don't take it back," he whispered, his lips now millimeters from hers. "Please. I love you too, honey, so much. I was afraid that because of Lindsay's attitude, you wouldn't be able to fall in love with me."

"No." Wrapping her arms around his neck, she all but jumped into his arms. "I would never hold that against you. Ever. I get she's upset because she lost her mom, and she feels like I'm trying to take her place, and I don't know if she'll ever get over that, but nothing could stop me from loving you. Nothing."

"Need inside you, honey. Now."

"You're the one with too many clothes still on," she teased, as he shot her a lopsided grin, then balanced her weight with one arm while he unzipped himself with his other hand.

Grabbing her hips, Grant lined himself up and then slammed home in one smooth stroke. Ashlyn cried out as he buried himself deep inside her, but it wasn't from pain, it was because having him inside her like this was perfect. It was everything she'd ever wanted, and even better than she had imagined sex could be with the man you loved.

Crossing to the bed, Grant kept hold of her hips as he laid them both down. His gaze never left hers as he began to thrust into her, and she clawed at his shoulders, needing him closer, as her ankles hooked around his waist, pulling him deeper in with every thrust.

"Love you so much," Grant told her as one of his hands reached between them and circled her bud.

"Love you more than I ever thought I could love another person," she whispered. Then Ashlyn took her bottom lip between her teeth, determined not to scream out her pleasure when his kids were just down the hall.

Which was harder than it seemed when he had her body spiraling toward pleasure.

When it hit, she just held onto him, riding out that wave of ecstasy together, the way she wished they could always be.

CHAPTER
Sixteen

December 4th
6:32 A.M.

"If you don't let me up, we're both going to be late to work and your kids will be late to school," Ashlyn reminded him, although Grant noted that she did little to pull herself out of his embrace.

"Maybe we should all take a sick day," he suggested. There was nothing he'd love more than to spend the entire day snuggled up in bed with this woman beneath him, listening to her breathy moans, her delightful giggle, and hearing her tell him that she loved him.

Damn, he could never get enough of hearing that.

After losing Lara, he hadn't thought he'd ever find love again, hadn't even thought he'd want to.

Until a stunning redhead in a killer black dress walked into her brother's wedding.

That night changed everything, changed him, and he didn't care that Ashlyn looked different now she was a blonde, and more often than not, dressed in jeans, she was every bit as gorgeous as she'd been that night.

Especially with Lindsay taking him dating so hard, knowing that Lara would be happy for him made falling in love with Ashlyn that much easier. Like he'd tried to explain to his daughter, there was room enough in his heart to love Ashlyn and build a life with her without taking anything away from his love for her mother.

"Let me up, you silly, goofy man." Ashlyn giggled, and he pressed his lips to hers for one more kiss before complying.

"Want to take a shower before we leave?"

"Nah. I'll shower at home. All my stuff is in my shower, and I may have quite a few products."

"Guess when we finally get married and move in together, we're going to need a bathroom with two showers, not just two sinks." Although Grant said it as a joke, he would be more than happy to have a large ensuite with multiple showers so Ashlyn could have all her stuff in one of them. So long as she was prepared to share the shower on occasion, the idea of her all wet and soapy had him growing hard.

Ashlyn was staring at him, frozen, half in the bed and half out of it. "When we get married and move in together?"

Smiling, he rounded the bed, took her hand, and pulled her up and into his arms. "Can't wait for that day."

A slow smile spread across her face. "Me either. I always dreamed of what my wedding would be like, ever since I was a little girl. I would imagine what my husband would be like, and how being married would be. But you, Detective Grant Bull, exceed every one of my dreams. Every single one. I love you."

"Love you back." Because he knew he really had to get to work and get the kids to school, he released her and stepped back. "I'll take a quick shower and meet you downstairs. Help yourself to anything in the fridge or cupboards."

"What do you usually have for breakfast?"

"If I have time, I usually just grab a couple of slices of toast."

"I'll make enough for both of us. Would the kids like some, too?"

"Lindsay usually has yoghurt, and Kevin cereal, but you can ask them if they want any."

"I don't want to overstep, but to give us a little more time, I could take Kevin to school so you don't have to drop off both kids. If it's okay, I mean. It's fine if it's not," Ashlyn hurried to add.

"That's fine, honey," he assured her, pleased that she wanted to step up for his kids. "Kevin will love going with you."

"You mean he'll love showing off my car to his friends," she grumbled, but there was no mistaking the gleam of pleasure in her eyes.

Giving her a quick kiss, he left her to get dressed and head downstairs, while he took a shower. Things with Lindsay might be the same as they were seven months ago, but in that time, Ashlyn and Kevin had bonded a lot. She was going to be everything he could have hoped for in a stepmother to his kids.

If only Lindsay could see that.

While he was trying to remain positive about the situation, Grant could admit that it was getting harder.

And harder when he heard yelling coming from downstairs.

Throwing on his clothes, he hurried downstairs to see that Lindsay had Ashlyn backed up against the counter. Ashlyn had been buttering toast when his daughter must have accosted her, and he had to give her major props because her tone was even when she spoke to Lindsay despite the teenager's hysterical screeching.

"Your dad said it was okay for me to drive your brother to school," Ashlyn said it like she'd already repeated this several times over.

"He wouldn't say that," Lindsay screamed. "You're not our mom and you're not family."

"I want to go with her, Linds," Kevin piped up from the table where he was eating cereal and scrolling on his phone.

"You're too young to know what you want," Lindsay yelled back.

"Enough," Grant announced, tone firm as he strode into the kitchen. "Ashlyn is taking Kevin to school because she asked, and I said yes. Your brother is fine with it, and it's not really your business. Besides, it means you and I can spend a little bit of one-on-one time together."

"You're really going to let *her* drive your *son* to school? Be alone with him?" Lindsay demanded, spinning around to face him.

"Yes. I am," he answered simply. "If Kevin had a problem with it, or was uncomfortable in any way, he knows he can speak up, and Ashlyn would understand."

"But—"

"No buts, Linds. The matter is closed."

Including all three of them in her glare, Lindsay stomped over to the counter and snatched up her backpack. "Then I'm walking to school."

"If that's what you want," he agreed. It would take her almost an hour, but if she left now she'd still make it in time for classes. Maybe she needed that time to cool down and get her head on straight.

Without another word, Lindsay stomped out of the house, slamming the door closed behind her.

"Sorry," Ashlyn immediately apologized. "I shouldn't have offered."

"Nah, she's just mad. I want to go with you," Kevin piped up before Grant could say anything.

More than that, Kevin got up, deposited his bowl in the sink, and then paused to give Ashlyn a one-armed hug, leaving her grinning after him as he sauntered off to pick up his game controllers and plop down in front of the television.

"Lindsay will come round, we have to keep believing that," he said as he pulled Ashlyn into his arms.

The problem was, he no longer believed it.

CHAPTER
Seventeen

December 13th
12:06 P.M.

It felt weird to walk in here alone.

All the times Ashlyn had been to Grant's house, he'd been with her. Of course, he had. This was his home, and she had her own place, so there was no need for her to use his spare key to let herself in.

Until today, anyway.

As she closed the front door behind her, she took a moment to pause in the foyer. She knew from talking with Grant that his place had been the first home he and Lara had bought together. It was easy to imagine what had led to them choosing the house, it was a great place to raise a family, and she wondered if or when she and Grant did get married, if he'd want to stay here.

With this house so full of memories of his past, she could imagine that he would, but Ashlyn couldn't help but feel like a fresh start might be better for all of them. No way would she object to their being pictures of Lara in the house, and she was sure there were other special keepsakes that Grant and his kids would want to keep. She didn't have any problem with that, but it would also be nice to have a clean slate, a place that wasn't his and his family's, and a place that wasn't hers, instead one that belonged to all of them.

"You're getting ahead of yourself, Ashlyn," she reminded herself as she hurried down the hall.

That was absolutely true.

Just because he'd mentioned to her, he wanted to marry her and live together didn't eliminate their biggest problem.

Thankfully, that problem was currently at school.

There were several meetings she had to attend this afternoon, one with a celebrity client who wanted to talk about their design ideas for a custom-made piece of jewelry, and the other with the board for a charity she was part of that had to discuss some problems with an upcoming New Year's gala. Really, she should be prepping for both, but when Grant had called and asked her to stop by his house because he'd forgotten to add the water to the bag of fake snow in his laundry room, Ashlyn found she couldn't say no to him.

"Because you're hopelessly in love with him and desperately praying that Lindsay will accept you, or at least stop being so openly hostile."

Sighing as she entered the laundry room, she found the huge paddling pool on the floor, with the fake snow powder inside. She couldn't really say she understood this thirteenth day of Christmas tradition the Bull family had, but both Grant and Kevin had been very excited by the fake snow angels they'd be making inside tonight.

Their excitement had been catching, and she'd agreed to be part of the fun. Knowing she got to spend another evening with her favorite guy and her favorite kid, had a smile chasing her worry away. Lindsay couldn't really hate her forever, surely. At some point the teen would realize that she was no threat to Lara's memory.

Adding water to the fake snow, when she'd filled the pool with the amount Grant had said, she stood for a moment and watched as the fluffy powder began to morph into fluffy snow. For something that was fake, it certainly looked realistic, and she decided the Bull family was onto something with these indoor snow angels. All the fun of real snow angels without the icy cold as wet snow seeped into your clothing.

Just as she was about to head out, she heard footsteps on the stairs.

No one was supposed to be there.

Grant was at work, and the kids were at school. Had someone broken in?

Moving as quietly as she could, Ashlyn grabbed the laundry room door handle and eased it open just enough to peek through, only to find there was no burglar.

Just one angry teenage girl who had obviously skipped school.

Slipping her cell phone, which she'd grabbed so she could call 911, back into her purse, she opened the door. Lindsay wasn't going to be pleased to see her, but she wanted to give the girl a chance to head right back to school before Ashlyn called Grant.

"What are you doing here?" she asked as she stepped into the family room.

Lindsay shrieked and spun around, her shock quickly morphing to rage. "What are *you* doing here? I live here, but you don't. Did you break in? Perfect, wait until my dad hears that you're some sort of psycho stalker. That'll get him to break up with you."

"Your dad knows I'm here, Lindsay. He called and asked me to come because he forgot to put the water in the fake snow. He told me where the key was hidden so I could let myself in. You're supposed to be in school, your dad won't be happy when he hears you're here, skipping classes."

"It's none of your business," the girl seethed. If hatred was a person, it would have to be Lindsay Bull.

"It might not be my business, but it is your dad's. I'm going to have to tell him." Not because she wanted to get the girl in trouble, but because she wasn't going to keep secrets from Grant. Especially not to do with his children.

"You're going to love that, aren't you?" Lindsay sneered. "Trying to get me in trouble with my dad so he'll like you better than me."

Surprise had Ashlyn's mouth dropping open. "I don't want your dad to like me better than you. Your dad loves you, and I would never do anything to change that. I just care about what happens to you, Lindsay, and you know better than to skip school."

"Shut up and get out," the teenager screamed.

"Talk to your dad, please, Lindsay. He's so worried about you, and this is only going to make him more worried."

"If he was worried about me, then *you* would already be out of our lives."

Staying was only going to continue to enflame things, so Ashlyn gave Lindsay a sad smile. "Your dad loves you more than life itself," she said softly as she headed back to the hall and out of the house.

Knowing she didn't have a choice didn't make the phone call she had to make any easier. Grant was going to be both angry and concerned, Lindsay was spiraling, and Ashlyn knew it was her fault.

Was it time to walk away from Grant?

For the sake of his daughter, she might have to.

Just as she pulled out her cell, she heard some sort of commotion inside the house. It sounded like something was knocked over, and then someone screamed. Was Lindsay throwing a tantrum in there? Trashing the place?

Another voice shouted something, and Ashlyn gasped. That was a male voice. Lindsay wasn't alone in there. She was skipping school with a boy, and it sounded like something was wrong.

CHAPTER
Eighteen

December 13th
12:27 P.M.

It was weird how the feeling of home could change over time.

When he and Lara first bought their house, for Grant, it was his oasis. Every day he couldn't wait to walk through the door to his wife's smiling face, whether he'd spent the day doing paperwork, comforting a sobbing victim, or putting cuffs on a violent criminal.

Home was home.

Bringing one little bundle of joy through the doors, and then three years later a second, had only added to that feeling.

But then he lost Lara and their third baby, and everything changed.

Home became a place he dreaded because when he was there, he drowned in memories of the woman he'd lost, and the life that they'd never share together.

In those early days, whenever he could, he got the kids out and about. The zoo, the library, museums, art galleries, the park, the beach, the local shopping mall, it didn't matter where they went so long as he didn't have to be swamped by memories of Lara.

But over time, things began to shift again.

Those memories were still there, but they became a little softer, a little sweeter, not quite so tinged with sadness and grief. The house began to feel like a home again, and he stopped trying to hide from it.

Then Ashlyn entered his life, she started spending more time with him and his kids, he fell deeper in love with her, and she began to feel like home. Only at the same time, he had his daughter growing angrier and more distant with each passing day, and his home began to feel like a battlefield.

The war they were fighting began to feel unwinnable, and he didn't know where that left him.

Walking away from his daughter wasn't an option, but walking away from Ashlyn didn't feel like one either.

"You look lost in thought," a voice spoke beside him, making him jump, and Grant realized he was standing at the sink in the precinct break room, filling up his mug to make a cup of tea, only the water was cascading down his hand.

"Yeah," he said with a weary nod as he shut off the water. "I am."

"Things with your daughter still not settling down?" Jessica Davidson asked. She had also been a single mom for years after her husband bailed on her and left her to raise their then two-year-old son alone. Freddie was now eight, and Jessica was no longer a single mom since she'd married Donovan last February.

Too bad his daughter hadn't embraced having a new parental figure the same way little Freddie had.

"No improvement," he answered, not sure quite how much Ashlyn had shared with her brother and sister-in-law.

"Being a parent is the toughest job in the world," Jessica said.

"Thought it was supposed to get easier as the kids got older. Instead, it's getting harder. What would you do? If you were in my situation?" Grant wasn't ashamed to admit he needed another parent to tell him he wasn't an utter failure for continuing his relationship with Ashlyn despite his daughter's objections.

"That's tough to answer, because every situation is different," Jessica hedged as he carried his mug to the microwave and stuck it in.

"It feels like I'm failing both of them. Lindsay and Ashlyn," he admitted.

"You're not failing either. You're trying to balance two conflicting sets of needs the best you can. If it helps, Ashlyn loves you very much, and she feels like you're supporting her through this. She just doesn't want to be the reason you lose your daughter."

"I don't want to lose either of them. Just feels like I'm stuck in an impossible position. Lindsay is still a minor, but she's not a child. She knows better than to treat another person the way she's been treating Ashlyn. But she is still a minor and my responsibility. I just don't want to teach her that throwing a tantrum is going to get her what she wants. In just a couple of years, she's going to be an adult, graduate, and go off to college. I want her to be mature enough to handle the adult world, and breaking up with Ashlyn just because she doesn't want me dating doesn't feel like achieving that."

Before Jessica could offer some words of wisdom, his phone began to ring, and he pulled it out, seeing Ashlyn's name on the screen. Despite the constant tension rolling in his gut, the smile that came to his lips was automatic as soon as he thought about the gorgeous blonde who had gifted him with her love.

"It's Ashlyn," he told Jessica as he answered the call. "Hey, honey, did you find the key okay?"

"Something's wrong," Ashlyn blurted out. There was real fear in her voice, and it reminded him of the day seven months ago when he'd saved her from being abducted, raped, and possibly murdered.

Snapping immediately into cop mode, he found himself already moving toward the door. "What is it?"

"I got into your house okay, and I put the water in the snow. But then I heard something."

"A burglar? Hide, I'm on my way."

"No, Grant. It's worse than that. It was Lindsay. She yelled at me. I tried to remind her how much you love her, but I knew it was best for me to leave. As soon as I got outside, I heard what sounded like her having a tantrum, yelling, and throwing things."

He sighed, wishing that he could say with absolute certainty that his nearly sixteen-year-old daughter would not behave that way.

Unfortunately, he couldn't.

"Then I heard a second voice, Grant," Ashlyn continued. "It sounded like a boy's voice, so I climbed the fence to get into your back yard so I could get a look, and I saw them. It's that boy she's been dating, I think he hit her, and now he's yelling at her. I can't hear what he's saying, but she looks scared."

The bottom dropped out of his world as he pictured his baby girl being hurt.

"I'm on my way," he assured Ashlyn.

"I'm going in, I won't let that boy hurt your daughter," Ashlyn said fiercely.

Seemed there was a second bottom in his world.

Because the thought of both his girls in the hands of a potentially unstable and violent teenage boy had him staggering under the weight of the fear.

"No, Ashlyn, don't. Hide and wait for me. I'm coming."

"Lindsay is your daughter. I'm not going to stand by and let her get hurt. I love you, Grant, please hurry."

With that, the call ended, and he took off at a dead run through the halls of the precinct, praying with a desperation he'd felt only once before in his life, when his wife bled out giving birth to their third child, flooding his veins.

CHAPTER
Nineteen

December 13th
12:33 P.M.

Bad idea or not, she was doing this.

Those were the same thoughts Ashlyn had nine months ago at her brother's wedding when she had her one-night stand with Grant.

Even if she'd known back then how difficult things were going to be between them, she would have gone through with it. Loving Grant was worth every second of trouble they'd endured because of Lindsay's hatred for her.

Loving Grant was also why this was easy to do.

Lindsay was his daughter, and he loved her with every fiber of his being. Going in there and protecting the girl was the only thing she could do. Despite his words, he'd never forgive her for standing by and watching as his daughter was hurt, while she cowardly kept herself safe.

Sneaking back to the front of the house, she tried to figure out how she was going to keep herself and Lindsay safe until Grant got there. The precinct was fifteen minutes away, and while he would likely also send the nearest patrol car, that could still be several minutes until anyone else got there.

Really, she was just hoping that her presence was enough to scare the boy off.

Stupid, maybe, but it was all she had.

Opening the front door, she called out immediately, pretending like she knew Lindsay was there, and Lindsay was expecting her. "Linds, I'm here, it's Ashlyn," she called out, and the angry voice she could hear immediately stopped.

Gathering every drop of courage she'd ever possessed, she continued down the hall and strolled into the family room like nothing was wrong. When she got there, she saw that three of the chairs from the kitchen table had been thrown and were lying in pieces on the floor, and the young man she knew only as Everett and had never met before, had Lindsay backed up against a wall.

Seeing the fear on Lindsay's face and the red mark on her cheek that would soon blacken into a nasty bruise shifted her protective instincts into overdrive. Lindsay may hate her, but the teenager was part of Grant, and Ashlyn loved Grant, so by association she cared deeply about this girl, too, one day she hoped to love her.

"What's going on?" she demanded.

"Is that her?" Everett sneered. "The woman your dad's dating? The one you wanted to get rid of?"

Get rid of?

Why did that sound a whole lot more ominous than just wanting to break them up when it came from the mouth of a teenage boy who'd just trashed the room and hit his girlfriend?

"It's fine, she's not so bad, my dad likes her," Lindsay mumbled, shooting her an apologetic glance, and she wondered if the teenager and her boyfriend had really discussed doing something drastic to get rid of her permanently.

Regardless, Ashlyn had chosen her path, and she didn't want to see Lindsay hurt worse than she already was.

"You need to leave, now," she told Everett. While she wanted him here to get arrested the second Grant or some cops showed up, her first priority was protecting Lindsay, and to do that, she needed the boyfriend out.

"Actually, Lindsay and I weren't finished chatting," Everett drawled.

"You mean you weren't finished beating on her," she corrected. "Lindsay, come over here. Now."

If she could just get Lindsay out of the room, she could figure out her next move, but right now fear for the girl was making it hard to think of anything else. Everett had already struck Lindsay at least once. She didn't want it to happen again.

"Actually, I think Linds is going to stay right where she is," Everett ordered when Lindsay went to move, and the teenager immediately froze.

When the young man pulled back his arm to hit Lindsay again, Ashlyn didn't think, she just acted.

Darting forward, she grabbed Everett's wrist, preventing him from striking Lindsay.

"Don't," she warned. "Don't do this, Everett. Don't make things worse than they already are."

Spinning around, he used her hold on his wrist to his advantage and reached his hand down to grab hold of her, breaking her hold and then throwing her against the table.

Ashlyn connected with it with a sickening crack, before sinking down to the floor, and pain spiraled through her body. She had no idea what damage he'd caused, but at least his attention was on her now and not on Lindsay.

"Run, Lindsay," she yelled, well, croaked was probably a more accurate term.

"Stay, Linds. This was what you wanted, wasn't it? To punish her for stealing your dad's attention and love?"

There was a manic grin on the boy's face as he closed the short distance between them, pulled back his foot, and slammed it into her ribs, and Ashlyn felt all the air leave her lungs in a rush.

"You wanted this, Linds, admit it. Tell her all about how you complained to me about her, bragged about how you were prepared to do anything to get her out of your dad's life," Everett continued as he kicked her again, in the stomach this time, and Ashlyn struggled to get her lungs to reinflate.

"I never wanted this," Lindsay screamed. "I never really wanted her hurt. I was just angry and wanted her to go away."

"We can make her go away now, can't we, Linds," Everett sing-songed. "A few more kicks and we might be able to get her ribs to just snap into pieces, pierce her heart or her lungs, and then bye-bye, new step mommy."

"No! Don't! Just stop, Everett, please, I don't want this. Stop, just stop." Lindsay sobbed.

"Can't stop now, we're having too much fun." Everett shot her another one of those evil grins as his foot slammed into her again and again until the world began to shimmer and fade, no longer quite staying in focus.

If she passed out, it was all over.

Not just for her but for Lindsay, too.

Because Ashlyn was pretty sure that once he finished her off, Everett was going to turn his violence on Grant's daughter.

The last thing she wanted was for Grant to get home only to find that she'd failed to protect his daughter and both of them were lying dead in his family room.

She tried to get up, failed, sank back down, and the next kick got her in the head, and it was lights out.

CHAPTER
Twenty

December 13th
12:40 P.M.

Rage clouded his vision as he stepped into his family room.

Grant had never felt fury like this before.

Anger, sure. When Lara had died, he'd been angry at the universe for taking her from him far too soon. As a kid, there had been plenty of times when he'd been mad at his parents and bickered with his siblings. As an adult, he'd been annoyed with his kids and irritated with his co-workers. There had even been times when a criminal he was investigating committed a crime so heinous that it filled him with anger.

But none of it compared to the fury flooding his veins as he took in the sight of his sobbing, hysterical daughter screaming at her boyfriend to stop, while Everett delivered another kick to a non-moving Ashlyn.

Was he too late?

Was Ashlyn already dead?

Had the universe taken a second woman he loved from him?

Since the kid looked unarmed, Grant didn't fire his weapon at the teenager, just launched himself across the room and tackled Everett to the ground.

The boy yelped in surprise, then turned angry brown eyes on him. That anger quickly melted into fear when he saw who had taken him down. Likely Everett had thought it was Lindsay, and that he'd be easily able to overpower her. But there was no way in hell that Everett could take on him and win.

While the need to pummel the kid was strong, Grant didn't want to waste time on the boy when Ashlyn was lying there, possibly dead or dying, at the very least unconscious and in need of medical assistance. Nor did he want his daughter to watch him beat up her boyfriend, even if the kid had turned out to be a violent psychopath.

Almost all of his anger was directed at the teenager he pinned to the ground, but a tiny bit of it was reserved for his daughter.

He'd heard what Everett had been saying when he burst into his house.

We can make her go away now, can't we, Linds. A few more kicks and we might be able to get her ribs to just snap into pieces, pierce her heart or her lungs, and then bye-bye, new step mommy.

There was no way he was ready to assess the possibility that his own daughter might have been complicit in Ashlyn's assault, even if that's what Everett's words implied. Grant had also heard his daughter's sobbed pleas for him to stop, that this wasn't what she wanted.

"You are under arrest," he snarled at the kid whose face had now lost all color.

Flipping the boy onto his stomach, Grant pulled out handcuffs and secured Everett's hands behind his back before shoving him to his feet. Ashlyn hadn't moved, she still lay about three feet away in a heap on the ground. Lindsay likewise hadn't moved, she was still standing, watching, tears streaming down her cheeks, her entire body trembling.

Torn between who to go to first, Grant decided on Ashlyn since she was unconscious. There was a darkening mark on Lindsay's face, but other than that she was okay. He had no idea if Ashlyn was as well.

"It's okay now, Linds," he called out, forcing his voice to come out calm when it was the last thing he felt. When he dropped to his knees beside Ashlyn, his fingers immediately touched her neck, praying for a pulse.

He couldn't lose her.

It would destroy him.

A second chance at love after losing what he'd always believed would be the love of his life was such a precious gift, and he wanted to treasure it until he was old and gray.

"Daddy." Lindsay sobbed, flinging her arms around his neck. "I didn't want this to happen. I swear. I didn't ask Everett to do this. I hated Ashlyn, but I didn't really hate her. I just needed her to be gone so I didn't hate myself. I don't want her to be dead. I never wanted her to be dead. I never asked Everett to hurt her. I just told him how I would do anything to make her go away. But I didn't mean kill her, Daddy, I swear I didn't."

Unfortunately, his daughter's carelessly spoken words were the flame that ignited Everett's violent rage.

Whether she wanted Ashlyn physically removed from their lives or not, the fact was her boyfriend had interpreted her words as permission to try to do just that.

Grant had no doubt that if he hadn't gotten there when he did that Everett wouldn't have stopped until Ashlyn was dead.

"She's not dead, Lindsay," he assured his daughter as he gently moved Ashlyn's body into the recovery position, since she was still unconscious.

"I'm sorry, Daddy. I'm sorry, I'm sorry, I'm sorry," Lindsay babbled as her arms wrapped around his neck, clinging to him in a way she hadn't since she was a little girl and needed him to banish the monsters in her life.

Today, the monster in her life had almost stolen something precious from him, and he knew that he was no longer prepared to tolerate Lindsay's rage toward the woman he was in love with.

"Therapy, Lindsay. You on your own, you and I together, the three of us, and the four of us," he added with a glance at Ashlyn's too still form. "I love her and I'm not cutting her out of my life. Not for anything. I don't want to lose you, you're always going to be my baby girl, but I love Ashlyn as well, and I'm not letting her go. You have to find a way to deal with it and accept it."

Expecting to meet resistance like he had for the last seven months, this time Lindsay just nodded. And when she looked down at the woman bleeding on the floor, there was a softness in her gaze that hadn't been there before.

"She tried to save me," Lindsay whispered through her tears. "Even though I've always been mean to her, she still tried to save me. Why did she do that?"

"Because Ashlyn is a good person, Linds. She loves me, and you're a part of me, which means that love extends to you as well. I told her to wait outside, but she said there was no way she was going to do that while you were in danger."

"She's going to hate me if she doesn't already. She almost died because of me." Lindsay actually sounded upset about the possibility of Ashlyn hating her.

"No," he told his daughter confidently. "Ashlyn doesn't have it in her to hate you."

But did Ashlyn have it in her to forgive Lindsay?

For seven months, all he'd worried about was his daughter not being able to accept his girlfriend. Now he was worried that his girlfriend might not be able to accept his daughter after this.

CHAPTER
Twenty-One

December 14th
10:02 A.M.

Everything hurt.

From her feet all the way up to her head, her body was just one great big throbbing mess.

Ashlyn knew she was lucky, though, knew things could have been so much worse if Grant hadn't shown up when he did. She had a concussion, three cracked ribs, some internal swelling and bruising, but thankfully, nothing that needed surgery. There was also a hairline fracture in her left arm. While she didn't remember it, she must have thrown up her arms to protect herself at some point, and Everett's kicks had broken it.

Waking up in the back of an ambulance, confused about where she was and what had happened, was not an experience she ever wanted to have repeated.

At least Grant had been with her.

His soothing words, even when her brain felt too muddled to make them all out, had calmed her, and the feel of his hand holding hers had grounded her when pain and fear felt like they were going to sweep her up and carry her away.

Most of the emergency room visit and subsequent scans and tests were a blur, and while she'd given a statement she hoped was mostly coherent to the cops that came to speak with her, and she'd spoken with Grant, she knew the details of what had happened, all she'd really done these last almost twenty-four hours was sleep.

Yet no matter how much she got, it never seemed like enough.

In fact, she was close to drifting off again when the door to her private hospital room opened. Grant had been by her side as much as he could be, and her mom and stepdad, and Donovan and Jessica, had taken turns keeping her company, but this was the first time she'd set eyes on Lindsay since they were in the family room with Everett.

Unsure what to expect, Ashlyn felt her body tense, sending a fresh wave of pain cascading through her. That set off the machines still attached to her to monitor her vitals, and Grant hurried to the bed. Lindsay remained hovering near the door.

"Shh, honey, you don't have to do this if you're not up to it," Grant soothed, taking her hand and bringing it to his lips to touch a kiss to it. "Lindsay asked if she could see you, and I said it would be up to you. If you want to wait, we both understand."

It wasn't that she was afraid of Lindsay, but there had been so much one-sided animosity that it was hard to be in the same room as the teen when she was so vulnerable.

Still, Lindsay was Grant's daughter, and she loved him with her entire being. That meant she had to find a way to make peace with his child if they wanted to have a future.

"She can stay," Ashlyn rasped, her voice still weak.

"Are you sure?" Grant's fingers were so gentle as they smoothed a lock of hair off her forehead and tucked it behind her ear.

"Yes." Better to get this over and done with. At least for once, Lindsay wasn't looking at her with hatred. The opposite almost. There was guilt, and sadness, and respect in the teenager's eyes.

"I'll wait just outside the door. If you need me, call for me." Grant leaned down and touched a kiss to her forehead, then crossed the room to the door. He paused, studied his daughter for a moment, then dropped a kiss to her forehead as well before leaving them alone.

For several seconds, they just stared at one another. Ashlyn didn't know what to say because she wasn't sure why Lindsay was there.

After a solid minute, Lindsay slowly crept toward the bed and stopped when she was beside it, wringing her hands together. "I talked to Everett about how desperate I was to do anything to get rid of you, but I never meant I wanted him to kill you or even hurt you. My dad said I have to do therapy, and that just sitting there and refusing to engage isn't going to cut it. He also said he and I have to go together, and then me, my brother, and him are also going to go together. He wants you to join us for some of those sessions."

Was therapy enough to fix this problem?

As much as Ashlyn would like to think it was, she wasn't ready to put her hope in anything yet.

"I told him yesterday, when he saved us, that I never really hated you, not really, it was just easier to transfer the hatred I was feeling for myself onto you," Lindsay admitted. "I didn't tell him why I hate myself, though."

Sensing the girl wanted to open up but was scared of being rejected, Ashlyn didn't speak, merely lifted her good hand and placed it over Lindsay's, which were still twisting together.

Tears rolled down the teenager's cheeks. "I can't remember her properly anymore. My mom. I don't remember the sound of her voice, or the smell of her perfume. I can't remember what her hugs felt like, and I can't picture her clearly in my mind anymore. I know those things because there are pictures of her and videos, and there's a bottle of her perfume I keep in a drawer in my dresser. But I can't *remember* them. It feels like losing her all over again."

"Even when those things get fuzzy, there's one thing you can't ever forget about your mom."

"What?" Lindsay asked, a hint of desperation in her voice.

"Her love. That love will always be inside of you. Nothing can take it away, not even time. Time can dull your memories, but when it does that all you have to do is remind yourself that your mom loved you with everything that she had to give. I don't ever want to take her place, Lindsay, I never did. I just want to love you in my own way, build our own relationship."

"I'm sorry." Lindsay wept. "I was so mean to you. I said terrible things, and some of them you never even told my dad about."

"He loves you," she said simply.

"I know. I know my mom loved me, too. I was just ... having trouble loving myself. I felt like a bad daughter, a failure, for not being able to remember my mom as clearly as I used to be able to. I took it all out on you. I wish I could go back, do things over. I wish I had listened when you told me you didn't want to take mom's place. I wish I had listened when Dad told me he loved you. I wish I had listened when Kevin said you were cool, and I should give you a chance. And I wish I had walked away the first time Everett put his hands on me."

Squeezing the teenager's hands, Ashlyn waited until Lindsay was looking directly at her. "You want to know something awesome?" When Lindsay nodded, she offered the girl a smile. "It's not too late to do all of those things. Everett is in jail, he can't hurt you again, and your dad, your brother, and I are all still here."

Ever so slowly, a smile curled up Lindsay's lips. "Not too late," she whispered.

"Not too late," Ashlyn echoed. Looked like maybe she was getting her Christmas miracle after all.

CHAPTER

Twenty~Two

December 25th
7:27 A.M.

Despite this Christmas season being one of the rockiest of his life, including even that first Christmas after Lara's death when he was only a couple of months into the grief journey and was juggling his job and a six-year-old and a three-year-old, the day itself was upon them.

Christmas morning was here.

Grant glanced over at Ashlyn, still fast asleep beside him. It had been almost two weeks since Everett beat Ashlyn into unconsciousness, and after she'd spent two days in the hospital, he insisted that there was no way she would be going home alone. After what had happened in their home, he and his kids had all decided they couldn't stay there any longer, despite the memories the house held of Lara.

They'd stayed in a hotel those first two days, but when Ashlyn was discharged, she invited them to move into her penthouse for as long as they wanted. Both kids had quickly agreed, and they'd actually had a nice day transferring all the decorations from the house to Ashlyn's place.

Actually, every day since the incident had been reasonably nice.

No yelling, no tantrums, no hostility, no drama at all from Lindsay. She'd been quieter, more withdrawn, but she'd walked up to him several times just to hug him and tell him she loved him. She'd also been going out of her way to do little things for Ashlyn while she was recovering, like carrying her plate to the table and making her cups of tea.

Was it too much to hope that a Christmas miracle had really brought them all closer?

"Morning, sleepyhead," he said as Ashlyn shifted carefully, still recovering from her injuries, and blinked open her eyes.

It took a moment for the sleep to clear from them, and when it did, she smiled up at him. "Merry Christmas."

"It is," he agreed. Sleeping in this huge king-size bed with the woman he was in love with pressed up against him, despite ample space for her to spread out if she chose to, was the most perfect way to wake up on Christmas morning.

"What time is it?" Ashlyn asked through a yawn.

"Seven thirty. Kids won't be up for a while if you want to go back to sleep."

"Actually, I'm kind of hungry."

Since it was the first time Ashlyn had actually had an appetite since she was assaulted, he was going to cook her the biggest Christmas breakfast ever. "Think we should make enough for the sleeping beauties to eat when they wake up?" he teased as he rounded the bed to help her sit up.

Ashlyn giggled, then winced, and he knew she was still in a lot of pain. A fact that made him want to simultaneously break something and get down on his knees and thank her for taking that beating to save his daughter.

"I guess since it's Christmas, we'd better," she answered as he draped her fluffy pink robe around her shoulders and helped her slip her arms into it before tying the belt around her waist.

Her cast-free hand slipped easily into his as they made their way through the gorgeous penthouse to the kitchen, where they both froze.

The room was a mess.

Ingredients were scattered across both the table and every available bit of countertop, the stove had three frying pans on it, the microwave was running, and two sheepish faces looked back at them from amidst the mess.

"Umm ... is this okay? We're cooking breakfast," Lindsay said.

"Trying to anyway," Kevin muttered.

"What are you two doing up this early on a non-school day?" he asked, surprised to see them making such an effort, well, Lindsay anyway. "Thought you guys wouldn't get your heads off those pillows of yours until at least nine."

"I woke Kevin up at six so we could cook, only it's taking a little longer than we anticipated," Lindsay explained.

"You guys are living here, at least for now. You're welcome to use the kitchen to cook yourselves breakfast or anything else you want whenever you want," Ashlyn assured them as he guided her to the table and pulled out a chair for her.

"Oh, breakfast isn't for us. It's for you," Lindsay told her.

"For me?"

"We wanted to surprise you," Kevin piped up.

"We thought we'd bring you guys breakfast in bed and then bring you our secret Santa gifts before we all went and sat around the tree and opened the rest of the presents," Lindsay added.

There was earnest sincerity in her tone, and Grant knew his daughter was trying her hardest to right her wrongs. It would take time, trust would have to be built, but Lindsay was trying. She had already attended two therapy appointments, and they'd had one with him and her, one with him and both kids, and one with Ashlyn joining the three of them.

Progress might be slow, but he didn't care. He wanted to build a solid foundation for their new family. One day, he hoped he and Ashlyn might add more children to the mix, and he wanted to ensure that when that happened, both Kevin and Lindsay were in a good place.

"We're not in bed, but we can do our secret Santa gifts, then eat here at the table," Ashlyn said, and Lindsay gave her a shy smile.

"Can we get our gifts now?" Lindsay asked.

"Don't see why not," he replied.

While the kids rushed off to their rooms, Grant grabbed the two small boxes sitting on the mantle behind them. They were supposed to exchange these secret Santa gifts last night, but Ashlyn had fallen asleep before they'd gotten around to it.

"I got Lindsay," she whispered.

"I got Kevin," he whispered back.

"I thought this would go badly when I picked her name, but now ... now I think it might help," Ashlyn added.

"I'm going first," Kevin announced as both kids came barreling back into the room. "I got you, Dad."

"No, I'm going first," Lindsay said firmly, holding a big box out to Ashlyn. "I'm sorry I would have messed up our first Christmas altogether if Everett hadn't ... you know. But I chose you a for-real gift, not the stupid prank I was going to pull. I hope you like it."

"Already know I'm going to love it, because you put some thought into it," Ashlyn said as she took the box and set it on the table so she could awkwardly, mostly one-handedly pull off the lid. "A planter basket with strawberry seeds in it?" she asked as she lifted it out.

"On one side," Lindsay said. "I thought maybe when they grow, we could use them to make those strawberry cinnamon scrolls you made me last summer. I never tried any, and you went to all that effort for me. To show me you cared. I didn't want to see it then, but I do now. If that's okay?"

"More than okay." Ashlyn reached for Lindsay and pulled his daughter into a hug.

"I thought we could maybe plant something you like on the other side of the planter," Lindsay added.

"Sorry, buddy, but I'm next," Ashlyn told Kevin with a laugh when he went to hand over his gift. "I got you, too, Lindsay. I hope you like it."

Handing over the gift box, she watched as Lindsay opened it and lifted out a Christmas ornament. There were painted angels around it, alternating larger and smaller ones, and it took him a moment to realize what they were.

"Fingerprints?" he asked.

"It took a bit of work, but I pulled a few strings and asked Jessica if she had any contacts who might be able to find a fingerprint on something Lara had touched. We got lucky, and they got one and scanned me a copy of it. I got Lindsay's from the prints taken when she was a baby, and I added the wings, heads, and halos myself. I know how much you loved decorating with your mom, Lindsay, so I thought this might be a special decoration to add to your collection. Your fingerprints side by side with your mom's, so you always remember she's your angel and is watching over you."

Bursting into tears, Lindsay wrapped her arms around Ashlyn's neck and squeezed hard. "Thank you, I love it. It's so much more than I deserve."

"We all deserve to be loved and forgiven when we're truly sorry," Ashlyn said, tears beginning to tumble down her cheeks as well.

Kevin rolled his eyes, but as Grant watched his daughter embrace the woman he loved, Grant wasn't embarrassed to admit his eyes were also feeling a little misty.

Can an apartment fire bring two hardened hearts together?
Merry Heat coming Christmas 2026

Merry Heat (Christmas Romantic Suspense #10)

Also by Jane Blythe

CRUSHED RUBY

FRACTURED DIAMOND

SHATTERED AMETHYST

SPLINTERED EMERALD

SALVAGING MARIGOLD

River's End Rescues Series

SOME SAVIORS CAN BREAK YOU

SOME REGRETS ARE FOREVER

SOME FEARS CAN CONTROL YOU

SOME LIES WILL HAUNT YOU

SOME QUESTIONS HAVE NO ANSWERS

SOME TRUTH CAN BE DISTORTED

SOME TRUST CAN BE REBUILT

SOME MISTAKES ARE UNFORGIVABLE

Candella Sisters' Heroes Series

LITTLE DOLLS

LITTLE HEARTS

LITTLE BALLERINA

Storybook Murders Series

NURSERY RHYME KILLER

FAIRYTALE KILLER

FABLE KILLER

Saving SEALs Series

SAVING RYDER

SAVING ERIC

SAVING OWEN

SAVING LOGAN

SAVING GRAYSON

SAVING CHARLIE

Prey Security Series

PROTECTING EAGLE

PROTECTING RAVEN

PROTECTING FALCON

PROTECTING SPARROW

PROTECTING HAWK

PROTECTING DOVE

Prey Security: Alpha Team Series

DEADLY RISK

LETHAL RISK

EXTREME RISK

FATAL RISK

COVERT RISK

SAVAGE RISK

Prey Security: Artemis Team Series

IVORY'S FIGHT

PEARL'S FIGHT

LACEY'S FIGHT

OPAL'S FIGHT

Prey Security: Bravo Team Series

VICIOUS SCARS

RUTHLESS SCARS

BRUTAL SCARS

CRUEL SCARS

BURIED SCARS

WICKED SCARS

Prey Security: Athena Team Series

FIGHTING FOR SCARLETT

FIGHTING FOR LUCY

FIGHTING FOR CASSIDY

FIGHTING FOR ELLA

Prey Security: Charlie Team Series

DECEPTIVE LIES

SHADOWED LIES

TACTICAL LIES

VENGEFUL LIES

CORRUPTED LIES

TRAITOROUS LIES

Prey Security: Cyber Team Series

RESCUING NATHANIEL

RESCUING TOBIAS

RESCUING MICAH

RESCUING JOSIAH

Prey Security: Delta Team Series

PERFECT REVENGE

Christmas Romantic Suspense Series

THE DIAMOND STAR

CHRISTMAS HOSTAGE

CHRISTMAS CAPTIVE

CHRISTMAS VICTIM

YULETIDE PROTECTOR

YULETIDE GUARD

YULETIDE HERO

HOLIDAY GRIEF

HOLIDAY LOSS

HOLIDAY SORROW

Conquering Fear Series (Co-written with Amanda Siegrist)

DROWNING IN YOU

OUT OF THE DARKNESS

CLOSING IN

About the Author

USA Today bestselling author Jane Blythe writes action-packed romantic suspense and military romance featuring protective heroes and heroines who are survivors. One of Jane's most popular series includes Prey Security, part of Susan Stoker's OPERATION ALPHA world! Writing in that world alongside authors such as Janie Crouch and Riley Edwards has been a blast, and she looks forward to bringing more books to this genre, both within and outside of Stoker's world. When Jane isn't binge-reading she's counting down to Christmas and adding to her 200+ teddy bear collection!

To connect and keep up to date please visit any of the following

www.ingramcontent.com/pod-product-compliance
Lightning Source LLC
Chambersburg PA
CBHW020730250626
47155CB00006B/2231